GW00801642

FINDING P!

JAMES LAWLESS

Indigo Dreams Publishing

First Edition: Finding Penelope

First published in Great Britain in 2012 by:
Indigo Dreams Publishing Ltd
132 Hinckley Road
Stoney Stanton
Leics
LE9 4LN
www.indigodreams.co.uk

ISBN 978-1-907401-78-7

Designed and typeset in Minion Pro by Indigo Dreams.

Cover design by Ronnie Goodyer at Indigo Dreams.

Printed and bound in Great Britain by: The Russell Press Ltd. www.russellpress.com on FSC paper and board sourced from sustainable forests

'I never pretended to offer such literature as should be a substitute for a cigar, or a game of dominoes, to an idle man.'

Robert Browning.

for Marguerite and Ava

FINDING PENELOPE

Chapter One

She hears the voice on the sand, gravelly and authoritative like that of her father's. Press the button and reject, that's me, she thinks, Penelope Eames, that's how I feel, or rather how I've been made to feel over the years, by him. Oh yes, the former esteemed professor of Histology and Morbid Anatomy with textbooks and learned articles to his name, who couldn't teach compassion or filial love. The early Spanish sun is lulling her, making her mull over things, things that she had decided belonged to the past now, to another country. The top of her left breast is burning slightly, the new red bikini being skimpier than her usual black swimsuit (she should have thought of that), and then the skin is more sensitive there after submitting to the knife. It was Sheila Flaherty, her agent, ironically who had suggested she go in and get the implants – her breasts were an average size. 'Good for your image,' Sheila had said.

She was reluctant at first, considering it a vanity to don the anaesthetic mask to undergo an inessential butchering of oneself (she never even put a tint in her hair, for God's sake). Sheila had had the job done a year ago, transforming her into the well-upholstered blonde that she now is. And for what?

For men.

Yes.

It was then they discovered the lump in her left breast. Quite young for that, the nurse had said, and Sheila tried to make a joke of it – 'you're the lump out and I'm the lump in,' and the nurse taught her breast awareness.

She hears the voice on the sand, the smoker's huskiness reeking of pseudo-wisdom; he thinks he is the cat's miaow. 'Not at all, my dears,' the voice (clearly English) is saying; 'on the contrary, chewing your nails is good for you; rich in protein you know. If I could reach my toenails, I...' Men, stupid old men, but maybe there is a humour there – who can account for taste? She looks up coyly from under her straw hat to locate the provenance of the voice: that elderly guy a few yards away with the silver ponytail sitting under a huge parasol in the canvas chair. He is holding forth with a bevy of young sycophantic beauties – just like him. Trying as he is to be youthful-looking like a born-again hippie or something out-of-date, just like him, the slate blue eyes, her father to a T.

Except of course for the ponytail.

The fine fawn-coloured sand she slides freely between her fingers, letting go, easing her life. She is delaying. The sun has made her lazy. She should be gone back to the quiet of her apartment to work on that recalcitrant second novel, before the sun reaches its zenith. She knows that, and to avoid the sunburn. There is a sound of laughter. She can just make out through the rising waves of heat: grinning young males (is the broad bronzed chap one of the lifeguards? She thought she saw him earlier on his perch) and two females among them playing volleyball as she gazes up into the sun from under the awning of her hand (for she has removed her sunhat which was chafing her forehead). She hadn't become aware of the net before. There are shouts in Spanish of 'Anda' and 'Olé' subsuming the elderly guy's utterances. The young men, in a veil of light and heat, are laughing at a monokini-clad girl who has just missed the ball. The putdown. What always emanated from her father. She wanted him to be proud of her as he was of Dermot, her younger brother, when he started on his science degree. Oh, such voluble praise. A scientist in the family. Mixing chemicals and potions in Quinlan's Laboratories. How right, how prophetic he was. And earlier her first book which she stuck at, she was sure he'd be proud of; she was hoping, her first novel to be published – but all he did was wonder if anything could be done about it, her writing that is, as if it were one of his studied pathologies.

Her right arm is going dead from resting on her side. She turns. Svengali of the bitten nails is calling the girls in from the sun. They are gabbling in different tongues – mainly Russian she thinks – among themselves, and in strained broken English to him. 'You'll sizzle up, my dears, out there.' She can see him clearly now as he looks this way and that, his ponytail bobbing like a pendulum. And the girls come running. And he sits on his chair like a king on his throne, his harem in the shade at his feet, and the blonde who had been playing volleyball without her top – the shameless hussy. It's a different matter to lie prone demurely in a topless state, Penelope convinces herself, with the towel on the ready to cover for any required movement, but to flaunt oneself in such a manner at sporting males, and he talking about fingernails... really! The girls are ignoring the taunts of the volleyball boys to come and play; they're concentrating on the mature man, positively drooling over him. Is he some rich dude? Is that it? They're after his money, or maybe he's a powerful film director – the chair, after all, in its canvas making could be interpreted as directorial. They're looking for parts; that's it, to be made famous in his next film. And the chrome-haired lecher pulls at the string of the nearest girl's bikini bottom.

Her father always called for Dermot, never for her when he wanted something, whether to announce or to confide, he made his bonding with Dermot. Dermot, the scientist, the proud son, the drug addict – pick the odd one out. Oh yes, Father did not know. In a moment of pique and green-eyed envy, which occurred when he called for him, she thought of telling her father, of releasing the cat from its miaow as it were, and of revealing to him what his whitehaired boy was really up to all those purblind years. The cocaine habit that started after their

11

mother's death at the in-set college parties, the social round of Dublin's elite (some of whom less canny are reduced like Dermot now ironically to the gutter). The mutual admiration society was what she called it, of all that talent and intelligence of neophyte lawyers and doctors and dentists and financiers, and scientists, a veritable whirl of brilliance in a newly vibrant country.

But he called for him, at the first sign of failing, for this junkie. It was like a dismissal to her, a rejection to one who had been tending to his needs all along.

All those needs. All along. All those demands. All her life. The best years.

And the last time Dermot came – Penelope had found him with the help of the drug unit in a down-and-out place: a lane, she can't remember the name of it – Crow's Lane, that was it, strewn with bottles and syringes and faeces and a pungent stench of urine which was trapped in the narrow street by overhanging buildings, so that, she mused, junkies would find their way home like animals by following their own smell.

Sometimes she wished her pain on both of them for all the years, not of material neglect – she was never left short in that regard – but for all the years of indifference. It must be the cruellest of wounds to inflict on someone, she considered, to do something unaware of or indifferent to the harm it would cause: to impose on one a habituation to worthlessness.

But – and she looks down at her wriggling toenails like a chorus to her thoughts – she is not worthless. She is a writer. She wrote to stitch the wounds, to seek affirmation from other sources. The great world out there.

She had her first story published in a teen magazine. 'Shows a lot of promise,' the editor had said. The story was about an orphan girl. What else could it have been about? she realises looking back, indulging the warmth of the Mediterranean sun at its height now (inducing her to linger). And then her first novel several years later, *Smelling of Roses*, a romance about the unfulfilled yearning of a young woman until she met the dark foreigner on a beach just like this one, feeding into what her father deemed the frenzied imaginings of impressionable females.

Men, she muses, as the waves beat rhythmically (she will venture into the water soon; she is sweating; she can feel the drops meandering into her cleavage). She was able to give up her job – her last job where she'd worked as a temporary tour guide in a Dublin museum, after a previous disastrous sojourn in a bank and an earlier stint at Telesales. She had wandered through an Arts degree but did not know what to do after it; had no one to guide her. 'Any dolt can get an Arts degree,' her father said, and that was the end of it as far as he was concerned. In contrast, she remembers some of her college friends with their careers mapped out for them by doting parents; the sang-froid of those young women, she marvelled at, as single-mindedly they pursued careers in the media or the diplomatic corps or later appeared in the society columns marrying some rich lawyer or dentist.

She bought an apartment on the Costa del Sol on the recommendation of Sheila ('Such a romantic country') from some savings she had, abetted by the royalties of her first book and the advance for her next one. A sequel, well not really, but in the same vein, more of the same, that's what they said, don't change a winning horse. Another love story maybe with a bit more umph this time, yes that is what they said. She could afford to be more daring in this second one – it is the twenty-first century after all, Sheila said, as if Penelope were not aware of that. Not exactly a bodice ripper no, we're not looking for that, but quality of writing and candour of expression, those are the things we are seeking in a novel for the independent woman of today, who is not afraid to venture forth et cetera et cetera. But there is a problem this time: Penelope's mind is in a flutter. After all, the first novel had been completed before her mother had died and before Dermot really went downhill. A mind needs, if not a stability, at least the semblance of it to write. She is thirty-three now, and has to think of her future. All the time previously, because of her father's conditioning of her (she blames that), she thought not of what she wanted but of what men demanded. But not any more. Better not to have got hitched at all than to painfully suffer afterwards as her mother had done – such acrimony, and she was a witness to it all. Penelope Eames had run the whole gamut of negative emotions before she left her teens, and without having to put a foot outside her family home.

She feels a palpitation as Mr Nails folds up his chair to make his departure. It's like she's missing him already in a sick sort of way, her father who is waning now, she has to admit, no matter what. She is afraid of loosening chains. Wanting and fearing at the same time. How had she come away? In what manner? The stubborn defiant 'Go if you must' of his followed by the demented 'Where are you off to?' And he refused to go into the nice nursing home in Booterstown which she would have arranged. To let someone else look after him, to take her place. But he would have none of it. Always winning the moral battle, to make the guilt hang on her.

Mr Nails has folded up his chair, his flapping gaudy shirt revealing a bush of wiry hair on his tanned, high-ribbed chest. He is moving away, the line in the sand filling in already from the mark of his chair as his seraglio disperses.

She must get back too, and forego the swim. But how to write, to concentrate, not knowing where Dermot is, her only sibling, her kid brother. She thought it would be easy, just a matter of coming away to leave such preoccupations behind her, but it's not so easy, she realises now; for such thoughts travel too and

14

find their own berthing. Dermot started his disappearance act after their mother's death; he would vanish for days, for weeks on end, and then reappear out of the blue with his dirty laundry and expect her to skivvy for him, while he chilled out, just as she did for her father. Penelope was caring towards Dermot; accepting it in the beginning with the way their mother was. Even to know where he is, no matter what travail he may be going through – it is self-inflicted after all. But it would be a relief; it would put her mind at rest, just to know he was all right, still on the straight and narrow where she had tried to place him before she left, for she could not in her heart have abandoned him callously in the condition she had found him in Crow's Lane. She brought him to the drug recovery unit on Merchant's Quay before he realised where he was going, driven there, she remembers, to the repugnance of the taxi driver. After a few days with her cajoling (the strain of it she still feels), and on a course of methadone, he slowly improved. She spruced him up in a tie and suit, got him a job, not the big scientific position, no, none of that now, but part-time work in a Supervalu off-licence. She knew the manager there who had worked with her in Telesales. It was all a rush but at least it was something to keep him off the streets before she departed for Spain.

The day she was leaving, she gave him her mobile phone number and her forwarding address.

'You're fucking off on me,' he said trying to make her feel bad, just like their father had done.

'If you ever want to come over...'

'Ha.' The sneer.

'I mean it, Dermot...'

But she didn't mean it, she knows, as she looks out on the crystalline water.

No, she has not settled here yet, despite the apparent

15

tranquillity of the surroundings: the rolling hills, the lenitive evening beaches sufficient to provide the balm but not the longed-for obliteration. But she is only a few days here after all; one must give time a chance to exact its healing powers. Her skin has hardly changed colour; she is still pasty-faced. Who used call her that? Dermot yes, pasty-face, he used to say, and he ironically always more pale than her. She intends to stay a full three months, at least, what Sheila had recommended. And who knows she may stay longer. Who can tell? She may even stay permanently; after all, who wants to go back to what she had left behind. But a full three months gestation period is needed to make inroads into a novel, Sheila had said, thinking it was her only reason for her move to Spain, for Penelope never revealed the intimacies of her family to her. Once that initial foray has been got over, Sheila told her, it can all be tidied up in gloomy old Dublin during the dark autumn evenings. And 'the bleak midwinter', Penelope adds mentally, finding masochistic consolation in the sadness of a song. And she looks now at the Spanish sky and is dazzled by the light. But – and a panic seizes her – she has made no encroachment, not even the slightest indentation on that carapace of the imagination, and nothing to constitute the happy ending that is de rigueur for her publishers. 'God knows,' Sheila said, 'there is enough misery in the world, without adding to it in our imagination. Write that blissful ending first, and then go back and recount the obstacles.'

So what am I to do? she wonders. What are the obstacles to happiness?

Her own life now.

She can't be worrying about Dermot. He's what? Twenty-five years old for God's sake this June, a full quarter of a century. And yet the words: 'I want out of it, I want out of it,' which he kept repeating in Crow's Lane, are haunting her now, the cry of his, rebellious but hopeless it seemed to her, that time she met him sprawled as he was in the slimy alley, calling out to the world that he wanted to get off. Oh, will he relapse into that state again? That is the fear that is haunting her. And, as for their mother, where was she during all of this filial malformation? She was on a metaphysical journey of her own incapability through a fug of alcohol and self-pity. An unloved woman, a woman scorned, the cruelty of the words hurled at her by her over-articulate spouse. How can one be over-articulate? No, but over-endowed with the bad words, the cutting words, the saw words that fell one. A woman betrayed many times, and she looks towards the sea and a girl dipping her crimson toes in the water's edge. Betrayed by his fawning acolytes who frequented the professor's room in the hope – in exchange for some momentary fleshy transaction – of summa cum laude in the examination. All done and dusted behind closed doors in those pre-PC days. She saw one such creature with her own eyes the day she went to summon her father when her mother had taken an overdose of analgesics – they didn't kill her, but they were an alarm bell. She remembers the rumpled girl, freckled blue-eyed, blushingly exiting, straightening down her skirt. Young enough to be his own daughter. To be her! And she remembers the monosyllabic dismissiveness of her father, 'What, what is it?' as she entered; the decoy of tidying his desk, lifting documents and placing them down in the same place again. 'Why did you not contact the secretary with such matters?' 'The secretary? About Mam, Daddy?' Did she not realise how busy he was, or could she not wait till he got home? Was it really that urgent? 'Not the first time.' 'Not the first time,' he repeated, that she had abased herself in such a manner. And there was an uncharacteristic dishevelled look in him too, she remembers, a Brylcreemed hair out of place, hanging tellingly over his high brow.

A volleyball lands near her, tossing up sand, forcing her out of her reverie. She hears Spanish boys shouting, 'Bravo' to a good smash. And as she stares, here he comes, the lifeguard (it is he) towards her, that handsome, young man in his cornflower blue togs with their yellow side stripes, and that quiff of raven hair falling like a wave so... so sexily over his right eye. He is what? in his late twenties, thirty at the most, just right for her to snatch him away if only in her imagination. She sighs as he stoops to retrieve the ball so unhurriedly, so maturely, unlike so many impatient young men, such as... yes, such as her brother. 'Lo siento,' he says. 'It's all right,' she says understanding the phrase. 'It's quite all right.' She smiles but is conscious of the tremor in her voice. And someone shouts, 'Ramón,' and he turns, answering to the name.

Chapter Two

Her apartment in the town of Felicidad is a two-bedroom unit on the third floor with a pine kitchen which she particularly requested rather than the standard cherry wood, and a horseshoe-shaped balcony, the front of which looks out on a communal pool, which she has yet to use, not that she is in any haste to do so, preferring to bathe in the sea to keep, as her next door neighbour Gwen says, her own bacteria to herself. And to the right of the apartment she is afforded that view, laterally of the sea, which is down a sloping road and near enough especially by night to be comforted by its primeval roar. A quaint fishing village, Sheila had said in her typical euphoria. She didn't say what year, for Felicidad is a cosmopolitan town now. And Penelope had purchased in good faith from the plans before the apartment was built. She had left it all to a lawyer, preoccupied as she was at that time with the promotion of her novel. Such little forethought, she acknowledges now, not without some regret, as she witnesses the erosion of those rolling hills with the mushrooming of tower blocks and all the big yachts crowding the newly extended marina. And there was no mention of noise near the diaphanous blue waters: the brain-shattering trepanations of electric drills, or the human cacophonies of an expanding population. Still, to be within sound and sight of neighbour she accepted of course, not wanting to be too removed from the social contact; such views and communal engagement, she realised she needed to ignite the spark of her imagination. And Gwen to the right, that is to say the side affording the sea view, of her balcony.

There are Russian and eastern European prostitutes – she learned that to her chagrin only later – who have taken up residence without any apparent legal opposition on the left side, which is to say the road side, of her balcony. Complained of to no avail by families who said they taunted their children on their way to school. She could picture it: painted tarts provoking the innocent like the world is undergoing a great corruption and our roles are preordained. They are just there waiting for the crime to happen. If she were Ruth Rendell or P.D. James, she imagines, she'd be willing it on, solely for the purpose of her work of course. But she, Penelope Eames, is categorised into the genre of romance (for evermore?) and she must look elsewhere perhaps; she must not cross boundaries or she knows she would incur the wrath of her publishers.

But she hadn't even focused on such things previously (no more than she had on the handsomeness of the lifeguard, until that moment...). And she considered another irony: a writer, an artist – although her father would have laughed at her calling herself that – so engrossed in herself, in her own little microcosm, failing to take stock of the world around her: the tottering of moralities, of old traditions, failing to witness a new unfettered universe unfold. She reaches under her matching red bath towel for her mobile phone, and texts Sheila – it's fine, it's easy to do, she's on Roaming. Sheila will be wondering how she's getting on. Once you get into it, Sheila said, the first one thousand words are the hardest. Funny, Sheila always saying that, presumably to all her clients, but she had that knack of giving the impression that you were the only one of concern to her with all that exhorting and advising, without her ever lifting pen to paper, except for editing purposes. And still – she felt her left breast sting not from the sun this time but from the memory of the knife – she owes a lot to Sheila, who had discovered her, who had promoted her, got her all those reviews in the press, and media interviews which really challenged her diffidence. She had to be pampered and cooed over by the redoubtable Sheila ('You can do it, Pen. You can do it'), and she was grateful to her, to hear a woman's words of affirmation undoing all the years, she is convinced, of paternal belittlement. And she knew – and that is why she fought to overcome the shyness – that without such promotions, there would have been no bestseller. So a little brief message to her mentor would only be right, to say she has settled in and started on her new book. Yes, how simple it is just to tell a white lie. And now she feels peckish and she ponders as she opens her wardrobe door: the little ivory number, if she could squeeze into that.

Chapter Three

She is sitting at a table for two in La Paloma Blanca. At a white linen tablecloth freshly laundered unlike the ubiquitous paper cloths that bedeck so many cheaper restaurant tables which are dotted around the town. She had discovered the place in a side street as she walked away from the commercial hub. It is not tackily touristy, but authentic with Serrano ham hanging from sharp steel hooks on walls. If food were displayed in such a manner at home, she would say it was unhygienic, but not here, no; here it fits into the ambience of the place like the heat as it competes with the electric fan whirring from the ceiling and the wine cellar in the corner and the keg of something or other just abandoned on the floor.

She's feeling fine after her shower and her new resoluteness. Her hair with its auburn sheen she was always proud of – one aspect of her at least which was universally admired – and there was nothing, not a thing her father could do to detract from that (but would it endure the ravages of sea water? she wondered; she must buy a good quality conditioner). But for now she feels its wavy texture as it hangs shoulder-length above her ivory cotton dress – another reason for self-affirmation, for she fitted into that dress without any difficulty whatsoever, despite not having worn it since last summer. Her waist has not changed as she still manages a size ten. She feels a pleasant tickling from the end-tips of her hair as it brushes against her neck and the pearl necklace which once was her mother's, and her mother's before her. Heirlooms provide the continuity, the anchor for those who break away. She sips her white Marqués de Riscal, waiting for the waiter to arrive with her lemon sole. She is tempted to have a cigarette which she is known to have recourse to in moments of stress, to complete the occasion as it were, but there is no reason for that, with such a good feeling possessing her now. She has been doing well considering, abstaining from that habit since she settled Dermot into what she hopes and prays will be some sort of regularity of life. Nevertheless, there is always an unopened packet of Marlboro in her black leather handbag – that soft calf leather which she is convinced that only Spain can produce. But she knows – and she finds solace in the knowledge – that the packet is there merely as a surety, just in case things ever became intolerable. She smiles, as a young waiter in a maroon-coloured waistcoat sets down her plate. The sole looks nice but much larger than she's used to at home.

'¡Qué aproveche!'

'Gracias.'

She remembered that phrase 'to enjoy your meal'. She must practise her Spanish more. She has the rudiments, self-taught from that Teach Yourself Book with the CD included which she bought when she decided to invest in Spain. The wine, she feels, as she replenishes her glass, is strong and mellow, filling her stomach with warmth. Like company. Ah yes, company. How everything is binary in this world. But she is not overly selfconscious, no; she is growing, she likes to feel, gaining in confidence. She is left to her own devices in this cosy restaurant. No staring males as on the beach. People are too busy with their own mastications. Still, is one ever happy? An odd male stare can do the heart good, like telling you you're still desirable.

And coming out of the restaurant swimmingly, swaying a little – boy, that wine was strong – she sees him under the light of a hunter's moon walking towards her: Ramón.

'Ah, you,' he says recognising Penelope as he draws near. 'I struck you on the beach with the ball, yes?'

'Not really,' Penelope says blushing slightly.

'No?'

'It was just a little shaking of sand.' Besides it wasn't he who had caused it but that awkward topless one missing the ball.

'Oh, still, I am very sorry from my heart,' he says stabbing his fist into his chest.

'It's quite all right,' Penelope says flattered by such an effusive demo of emotion. 'No harm done.' (What an inane statement, she realises too late. No harm done).

'Please allow me to... buy you a drink.'

'Oh, there is no need. I've just...'

'But I insist. A little something.' And he is already wheeling her towards an outdoor table where a candle flickers in a gentle breeze.

'And your name?' he says holding the chair for her.

'Penelope,' she says.

'Ah, like Penelope Cruz. She is my favourite actress. You should go and see her film, Volver. It is showing in the Centre.'

'Maybe I will.'

He summons a waiter. 'What would you like?'

'A cup of tea.'

'A cup of tea?'

'Yes, please.'

Oh how she would've loved, as his soulful eyes shone in the candlelight, to have said Sexonthebeach right there and then.

Chapter Four

She walks through the streets towards her apartment oblivious of the crowds going out for their Saturday night revels. Her mind is suffused with him. He had offered to walk her home but she said it was not far, that it was all right and, what she liked about him was he did not press her. But he has done something to her. Touched her like a demon lover. No, not a demon, but touched her nonetheless, somewhere intangible in her deepest self; like he's lit a flame inside her. How strange that people can instil such a feeling of beneficence in another, and she thinks of her father, and its opposite. Oh, it's easily done. But he's not here now to put his dampener on her feelings, she realises, as she dovetails in and out of passers-by, of raucous teenagers in the main; how like birds they are in their flocks with their shrill-pitched crowing. She can think of him, Ramón. How dashing he looked in the half light in his short-sleeved white cotton shirt, enhancing his dark features. And the shirt so perfectly ironed – did he do it himself? (Something her father or Dermot would never conceive). Oh to graze the smoothness of his skin, to drink in the kindness of those peat-brown eyes, more apparent then in the flickering candlelight, in the off-duty revelation of the real man beneath the brawny exterior, exuding sensitivity. And such politeness, holding the chair for her as he did.

She, despite the tea, is still feeling a little tipsy from the wine, and conscious of swaying. No, it is not swaying; it is just a stepping out of someone's way – that bleary-eyed child with the ice cone. Penelope was always in control, of her physical propensities at least; she took pride in that, unlike her mother, as she feels the pearls on her neck, the falsity of their symbol; or her brother too, for that matter. What is it like to soar without any reins to pull one in? The thought fills her with apprehension. She passes tourist shops still open, assistants putting in long hours peddling wares to mainly middle-aged couples (the younger ones are ignoring the shops and, painted up to the nines, are shrieking all the way to the discos) with flipflops on the women and straw hats and some still in bathrobes camouflaging their swimsuits. They scrutinise souvenirs: ashtrays, trinkets, necklaces and earrings with zirconia stones. She passes by the blue sign (what sort of blue?), the gentian violet neon of La Caverna. Would she go to a disco? Would she venture in? It's been a long time since... A queue is forming and two bouncers in their bounden black are standing at the door which looks like a vortex with its tunnel shape ready to suck one in. She looks towards the bouncers who, it seems to her, are vetting more than their remit as they gawk beyond the queue at the young females passing down the street. One of the bouncers catches Penelope's eye and throws her a loud vulgar kiss. 'Hola, guapa.' And he beckons with a flourish of his hand for her to enter. She averts her eyes and walks on.

Someone is shouting up the street. A tall man in a tam-o'shanter and encased in sandwich-boards, is handing out cards for Paddy's bar: two drinks for the price of one. A place to be avoided, she decides; may as well be at home as go in there, for tribal gathering or noble calls for homesick blues. The night is young, she repeats and she realises she is sounding like a heroine in a novel, thinking the world romantic. Oh, she fully intended to make another stab at that first chapter. To get through that fog, she concluded, would enable her to be on her way in the morning sunshine on her balcony ready and bright and cheery. Was he asking her to go to the cinema with him? That time he mentioned the Centre? But not tonight. Fatigue was there – from the sun and the sea and of course from the alcohol. She therefore told Ramón that she must return to her apartment, that she was feeling... '¿Cansada? Ah yes,' Ramón had said with such empathy

26

in his eyes. She thinks of her mother, the real reason perhaps why she was always reluctant to let herself go. She could never bring herself to love her, to love such a person who was so weak-willed, not only in her drinking, but also in the neglect of her appearance especially with her hair; she remembers the growing infrequency with which she washed it, as if there was no need any more, that she was beyond caring. Not that she despised them, her mother and her brother; despising after all was her father's domain. It was more an anger she felt towards them for allowing themselves to be subjugated, to be in thrall, as both she and her son were with their respective dependencies.

There are late swimmers (more adolescents) still shouting and splashing in the pool as she arrives at her complex. She passes through the bar where a group of young adult males and one out-of-place female are seated on high-legged stools shouting at a television set. 'Real Madrid,' someone exclaims with an English accent, as she presses the button for her lift.

It's a balmy night. One could hug oneself with the feeling it exudes; not overpowering like the day was. She places her laptop on the balcony table with its glass top and stares at the stars and the bright moon like a lantern lighting up the sky and diminishing all those garish dangling artificial lights down below. Are they left on all night? She never considered that. She can make out the Plough, so clear. But enough! She steels herself to concentrate and, disdaining the urge to make a cup of tea (another cup?), presses open the lid of her laptop. The noises from the pool have subsided; just the sprinklers are to be heard now on the lawns like cicadas sounding. Someone has started singing in the bar, a booming ballad, but that in time fades too. She types, just words that come into her head to get a flow. Get anything down, Sheila had said. And soon she has a rhythm, and

27

words and phrases and sentences even are looming and gelling before her eyes on the liquid screen, as if they are separate entities from herself, divorced from the action of her fingers. She hears a sound, the door opening of the adjoining apartment. The door closes. There are voices, muffled, difficult to make them out: a couple of words in shrill foreign accents, and then the voice in English, haggling over a price. She turns sideways to look towards the lighted window: a tall blonde in a skimpy red skirt appears and pulls down the blind.

Chapter Six

Penelope throws back her bed sheet as the sun is rising and beaming in at her through her balcony window and she feels that wonderful life-affirming heat, so cheering, unlike that dreary drizzly so-called summer weather she left behind in Dublin; another reason to justify her staying, she convinces herself. She breakfasts lightly, not through any conscious effort of reducing; no need, but would that always be the way? Would she in time grow bloated too like her mother, and she with a particular puffiness around her eyes, those self-pitying globes that looked like they were going to burst into tears at any moment (she had a weeping left eye owing to some duct problems which augmented her appearance of sadness). No, she is more – and she hates to admit it – like her father in her gaunt ways. She sets the table on her balcony, still wearing her salmon pink cotton pyjamas; she never – and she gives a little wriggle because no one can see her – paraded around the house like that at home. Even as a child. Could you imagine it? What her father would have said – decorum being his pretence of course. And here she is now on a balcony in public view and he can sod off. It is, she feels, showing the nonchalance of a person growing more comfortable with herself, with her own body, the freedom engendered by distance. She sits at her balcony table to settle into an orange juice and tea and a croissant semi-hard which she'd bought yesterday on the way home from the beach. The temptation strikes her to go out to the panadería or is it the pastelería? and buy fresh croissants. She's a Kellogg's Special K girl when at home, but found the packet too bulky to fit into her suitcase. Maybe they sell it over here; she hadn't spotted it as yet in any of the shops. She misses it though; funny, after only three mornings; apart from cereal, she missed that auburn-haired girl in the red swimsuit on the cover, sitting at the edge of the swimming pool dangling her feet, that Sheila said was the spit of Penelope. That's what prompted her to go out and buy (not the cornflakes; she chuckles), but a bikini of the same colour. To draw the image closer. So if she were writing a book, which of course is what she is doing, if she were describing herself as a character, she would simply refer the reader to the girl on the special K cover to furnish a clear picture (worth a thousand words) of her. But she is not a painter; she is a wordsmith and she must get down to work. Anyone would think she was on a holiday the way she was going on, such dawdling. There must be an ascetic code to the artist, she tells herself, for time she cannot afford to fritter away. Maybe tomorrow as a special treat, she would pop down to that panadería, but only if she gets some work done today.

The sun enhances the turquoise blue of the pool below, making chlorinated water look good, camouflaging bacteria, she ruminates, as she gazes over her balcony. It's all right, she tells herself, just settling her bearings before she starts. A couple of early, elderly sunbathers (the younger set, she presumes, are still undercover nursing hangovers or whatever) – a square hulk of a man and a bronze-tanned woman – are setting up towels. Are they German? she wonders, or is it all a myth about their early rising and claiming reclining beds with their towels while they go off and have breakfast? After all they are blonde, but they could be Swedish or any nationality for that matter these days, with the dyed blonde look in vogue universally now and indeed for both sexes; and besides, as a writer she realises she must not enter such a world of stereotypes. Two huge books act as weights on their towels. What books? she wonders. Large colourful tomes that look like sandwich boxes from up here. The pool is still and silent with an air about it, she feels, of expectation with the early sun glinting on it, and those garish lights that hang all around the pool in competition with the moon last night, are turned off now, and their presence is almost invisible in the light of day, except maybe when a little breeze blows to dangle their wires. She clears her croissant plate and returns her orange juice carton to the fridge and moves her glass table to a shady corner of the balcony. She sets her tea – her second cup – down and starts to type.

The door bell rings.

'Penelope.'

'Gwen.'

Gwen is a small woman somewhere in her forties with a big round face, like a clock, Penelope thinks. Her sunglasses are propped, almost concealed, in the purple of her tinted hair; and very English in her summer floral dress, rather out of date, making her look like an older generation despite... well she is older generation, but like a lot of expats on the Costa who seem, at least fashion-wise, to be trapped in a time warp and, contradictorily, try at all costs to prevent the impression of ageing. More cosmetic jobs are done on Costa inhabitants than anywhere else in Europe, she had read that. Gwen had jobs done, it was clear to Penelope, on face, chin, neck, but she doesn't blow about it like Sheila does. 'So you finally got here?' 'Yes.' Gwen is holding a green plastic bag with El Corte inglés repeatedly printed on it. 'You were shopping,' Penelope says. 'I was in Málaga. It took an age to get back. The four o'clock bus, you know what time it arrived? Twenty-two minutes late. Spanish transport,' she says, and in the one breath, 'It's only when I returned, when I heard your table scratching on the balcony tiles, I realised you'd arrived.'

As they pass into the hall, Gwen says, 'The painting.' Penelope fixes on a square of cerulean blue, slightly brighter than the rest of the wall. 'It's gone.' 'I noticed it too,' lies Penelope, 'the first thing when I arrived. Someone must've taken it when I was away.' 'Well, I never. Who would do such a thing?' says Gwen clearly disappointed. 'Could it have been one of the cleaners, or was there a workman in? Spaniards, you know,' Gwen says. She had bought the painting for Penelope, as a house-warming present. It was an inferior mass-produced copy of a sailing boat on the horizon of where? Of nowhere, Penelope decided. There were no specific demarcations, no familiar area one could identify; it was just an abstract nonentity produced from a machine rather than from the heart. Penelope hated the painting and had disposed of it discreetly. Besides, she thinks, reinforcing her argument, arbitrary and subjective things like paintings chosen by others are tricky enough at the best of times, like intrusions into one's own private aesthetic. It was like, she felt, here is Gwen, prescribing taste for one like an old English overlord with subterfuge colonising one's pad. Penelope wanted her apartment to be her own, to be free of the influence of others; that was the purpose of her buying it in the first place. Surely Gwen, the unwitting, the non-connoisseur of art, could have bought her something else if she had a mind to buying her anything at all. She had noticed it in Gwen's own place, all these cheap tacky supermarket pictures festooning her walls, which Gwen thought were wonderful. 'You'll have to paint the wall again,' Gwen says resignedly. 'I know, I know,' Penelope says. 'There's so much I have to do.' 'Until such time as I get you a new painting.' 'There's no need for that.' 'It's no trouble,' Gwen says. 'Next time I'm in that hardware store I'll pick up another one for you. Would you like one maybe with horses next time? I'm sure I saw a pretty one with horses.' 'That would be nice,' Penelope says, 'but anyway, Gwen, I must apologise. I'd fully intended to call on you. I've been trying to work on my book, you see.' 'Oh, a new one?' 'Yes. Now come on,' Penelope urges, 'we'll sit out on the balcony.' 'I hope there's going to be plenty of humour in your new book. A good laugh is what's needed around here. I'm looking forward to reading that.' 'You'll be waiting a while,' Penelope says adjusting her hat to counter the rays of the sun. 'Do you want a hat, Gwen?' 'What, and lose my light under a bushel?' 'I've only started,' Penelope says. 'That's why I came to Spain this time. I thought maybe I could make some progress on it here. No...' – she was going to say distractions – but thought that Gwen might take that personally – so she says, 'no family here to interfere.' 'Ah ha, family,' Gwen says, and Penelope waits for her to elaborate, but all she says is, 'I've brought some croissants,' and she proceeds to take them out of her bag.

'Well, tell me,' Penelope says as she pours boiling water over cringing tea bags in two tall green mugs. 'You don't want butter on that?' Gwen is already making incursions into a croissant. 'No, jam usually is what I put on them,' 'Don't have any. Didn't get around to...' 'Never mind. I'm watching my weight anyway, or trying to.' She sighs. 'Not making a good job of it, am I?' she says holding her tummy. 'You look fine,' says Penelope, thinking her floral dress is a good disguise, except for her bare freckled upper arms which she has to admit appear a little more bloated than last time she saw her. 'Any news from Aubrey?' Penelope says. 'Oh, that's all fixed up. About time too. Four years of wrangling over entitlements.' Aubrey, she knew from Gwen, had money; was a successful London businessman, into stocks and shares but slow to pay out seemingly, to settle the divorce. 'He's whizzing around the green fields of England in his Lamborghini with that flaming redhead of a young secretary at his side, tickling his vanity. That's what men want, isn't it? They like to have their vanity tickled, and the thing is when you don't comply, when you get fed up with it all, they say cheerio and look around for a younger plaything. That's Aubrey, the balding, for you now. Oh dearie me,' she says and stuffs another piece of croissant into her mouth. 'But at least I'm free now.' 'I'm glad,' Penelope says. 'I'm open to offers though,' she says hooding her eyes coquettishly.

Penelope blushes, feeling the pause between them uncomfortable. 'Drink up your tea,' she says, 'it's going cold.' 'Ah yes,' says Gwen sipping. 'Aubrey was someone who could colour your view of men for life.' 'You don't really mean that?' Penelope says and the thought of her father crosses her mind. 'Oh I do,' Gwen says breathing in, drawing Penelope's eyes towards her enhanced bosom. She's not wearing a bra, Penelope realises. Still, nothing odd about that in a hot country. 'But I still party,' Gwen is saying, 'only with the expats of course. What some of them get up to,' and she throws that look again towards Penelope who, despite herself, is forced to cast downwards, 'would quite surprise you. In fact, what day is tomorrow?'

'Friday,' says Penelope.

'It is Friday. I'd almost forgotten. Would you be up to going to a party?'

'Where?'

'In Charlie Eliot's villa.'

'Oh I don't know, Gwen. Who is he?'

'You don't know Charlie?' Gwen says. 'Everyone knows Charlie.'

The words she types on the VDU, what are they? They're not feel-good stuff, that's for sure, that is oozing out of her head. They are of sadness, words of loss, of fathers, brothers, mothers, all the people lost. The world was made round so we can't see ahead. What is this? she wonders. Is she going through a depression? Is that what has been wrong with her all along? Only now revealing itself through the creation of words. It is because of Dermot, she knows that. Where is he now at this precise moment? she wonders. Is there any hope for him? Many drug addicts recover; lots and lots; their stories are all over the tabloids every day of the week, a feel-good story, what people want: how I came back from hell, that sort of thing. She rests her hands at the sides of the keyboard. Could she have done more to help him? The guilt; it is worse over here, despite the contrary expectation that distance would rid her of such feelings, interlaced as it is with absence and loneliness and helplessness. She can't enquire. Still in a huff with her for going away, he had refused to give her the number of his mobile phone. Is he sticking at the off-licence job? Is he going to the group therapy classes she recommended? Oh, what if he has lapsed again? She can't go and search for him anymore in the back lanes of Dublin. He is beyond her reach from here. And that's what's blocking her now in her writing. But it is not a block; it's a different direction her writing is taking; she must go with it, let it lead her to wherever. She writes:

A young woman is hurrying down a dark sidestreet. It is raining and her hair is matted. She is scared. She can't find a way out of the street. There are no side turns. There are doors along the walls all padlocked. The street has no end; it keeps going and going like a train tunnel, and...

Her mobile phone rings, startling her, that loud William Tell overture. She must change it; it's too over the top. It's Sheila, responding to the text message, wanting to know how she is getting on, which translates as how is the novel progressing? Sheila is not one for heart-to-hearts, which is what Penelope longs for at this moment. Even her talk of her breast implants was scientific and boastfully libidinous. Sheila is unflappable, which is, Penelope admits, what she has to be to be a good agent, and she is that. Getting on? 'I'm getting on fine,' Penelope says. 'Yeah? You sound hesitant.' 'No no, I'm fine honestly. You caught me in midthought, that's all.' 'Oh sorry about that, Penelope,' Sheila says. 'I hope it wasn't a climactic moment.' She gives a hoarse laugh. Is she still smoking those cheroots? Penelope wonders, to complement the dark trouser suits she is fond of wearing. 'No, you're fine.' 'You're well into it then, I take it?' 'Well...' 'The first chapter, the magic first thousand word hurdle surmounted?' 'Well, nearly. I'm doing a bit of planning at the moment, plot structure you know, just to get it right before I plunge in.' 'That a girl,' Sheila says. She hears the flicking of pages of what she knows is Sheila's yellow ring-backed notebook. 'I have a few things lined up.' 'But I...' 'Just to have things ready you know, keep you in the public eye after the success of Roses. We don't want anything to flag now, do we? I'm keeping their interest on hold. All those readers. Nothing like a bit of suspense, eh Penelope? One on radio three and one with Tiffany.' 'Tiffany?' 'You remember Tiffany Pringle who gave you a good review in *The Female on Sunday*?' 'Oh yes.' 'Well she's anxious to do a full length profile of you. Is that good news or what?' 'Oh yes, that's very good news.'

Oh God, this is what she dreaded. How can she do an interview after what has happened with her father and her mother and with Dermot the way he turned out? What can she tell this journalist about them? Some novelists, she realises, have no qualms in that area; take positive delight in fact in revealing family privacies, warts and all; are even known to embellish matters to their own advantage. Oh, she's read some of those so-called memoirs, in many cases their coloured accounts paying little heed to the pain they may inflict on the rest of the siblings. She is not one for that: gaining sympathy from the reader by fair ways or foul, the ego drawing the reader to her person as much as to her work. The work, she is beginning to realise only now, should be paramount, should not be subsidiary to the person. But tell that to the media people. Isn't it quicker and easier and more lucrative to read about the scandals of artists than to struggle through their tortuous prose?

She thinks of her mother and the deep-rooted burial of subconscious things. Would that sort of subliminal stuff surface, escape through the leaks in her own self-confidence? What Freudian slip would she make? The last time, for her first novel, the excavation had not yet begun. But now she is Penelope Eames, public figure. The package, as Sheila says.

'Penelope, are you there?' 'Yes, sorry.' 'The line must be bad, but listen, there's the possibility that she could go over, I mean do the interview from over there.' 'No hurry,' Penelope hears herself saying, 'give me some time on that.' 'Time to get a good suntan, right? To look your best, not that you don't always look ravishing. We have to maximise your potential, don't we? They'll want photos. That's what they all want now, poses of young sexy authors. That's what sells the books.' 'Sex, I know,' Penelope says unconvincingly.

'Oh, and another thing I was thinking,' Sheila says. 'What?' 'Now that you're over there...' 'Out with it, Sheila.' 'In Spain I mean. Why don't you pen a couple of hundred words on the expats?' 'The expats?' 'Yeah. Why not? You know it could even feed your novel with a few extra ideas. Who knows it could even

37

give it a new dimension. And who would you have to thank?' 'You, Sheila.' Sheila laughs gratifyingly. 'Ha ha. We could use the article. I could get it into a few of the chic magazines for promotion; some of those glossies they read on the beaches you know; may even get it into Cara.' 'Cara?' 'The Aer Lingus in-flight magazine? Yeah, why not? It's relevant and topical and will keep you in the public eye. All those holiday makers going back and forth spreading the news. Remember a bit of romance blooms there too in those circles, I'd say.' 'Actually, Sheila,' Penelope says, 'I am invited to a party. So, I may be able to do something.' 'That a girl. Remember, keep the romance in the air. And don't forget the bit of umph. Frills and Bloom are not what they used to be, you know. They're coming out of their closet now, believe you me. And the happy ending, don't forget. That's a constant.' 'I know.'

Penelope sighs. Is Sheila's life really like this? she wonders. Does she possess all those ingredients of the romance novel? Does she have a happy ending every night going to bed? 'We always have to keep the end in mind, don't we?' Sheila is saying. 'Yes, we do.' 'What your readers want.' 'Now you've said it.' 'You're building up quite a fan club, you know.'

Where? Penelope wonders. Three letters and seven emails were all she received in the wake of the success of her first novel despite its commercial success. 'And positive vibes, remember.' 'I remember,' Penelope says. 'That feel-good factor, that's what makes your readers into lifelong fans. That's what you're after, cherry pie.' 'Of course,' Penelope says, 'I'll get working on it.' 'It was a good advance,' Sheila says. 'It certainly was.' 'Had to do a lot of wrangling.' 'You did that,' Penelope says, 'and I'm grateful.'

She has been here before listening to Sheila looking for kudos for all the work she has done. 'Penelope.' 'Yes, sorry Sheila.' 'So things are good over there then?' 'Oh yes, things are fine. The beach and the sea and the sun. I have no excuse.' 'Buying that apartment was a good move. I told you, didn't I?' 'Spot on,' Penelope says. 'And you're eating well?' 'Oh yes.' God, she sounds like a ward matron, or for that matter a non-dysfunctional mother solicitously quizzing her child, and Penelope thinks of the lemon sole and the Marqués de Riscal she indulged in the previous night. 'I hope men are on the menu,' Sheila is saying. 'Well.' Penelope laughs. 'We'll have to see.'

Gwen calls for her at eight in what Penelope considers to be a far too revealing number – her boobs are practically popping out of the low cut black dress. 'Not for me, dearie, the Over-The Shoulder-Boulder-Holder' she says to Penelope's involuntary gape, and a matching handbag hangs from the crook of her arm with sequins that shine in the last rays of sun fading from the balcony window.

Reeking of perfume, Gwen, unasked (she was managing quite well thank you, receiving as she was up to this her instruction from the wardrobe mirror behind her), helps Penelope tie the back of her halterneck red dress, her fingers lingering at the strap, to play a piano tune on the bare part of her back.

'It's a lovely dress,' Gwen says stroking the hem as if to smooth it down.

'You think it's all right?'

'It's fine,' Gwen says, 'but you need to get working on your tan. You're so pale.'

What about past ages? Penelope wonders when to be tanned was a peasant quality frowned upon, and pale skin, the milk white epidermis of a Cleopatra, was a sign of class.

'I've a taxi ordered,' Gwen is saying.

'Is it far?' Penelope says.

'Less than half a mile. You weren't thinking of walking, were you?' Gwen laughs, that high-pitched breathless giggle.

'I wouldn't have minded,' Penelope says for the evening outside looked mild now and welcoming.

'Not in these,' Gwen says and both women look down at Gwen's leopard print platforms rising off the ground, making her almost touch heads with Penelope now. But such small feet. What size? A three perhaps, like a child's.

'Do we have to bring anything, like a present I mean? The party, it's not in aid of anything, is it?' Penelope says as they go out the door, her shampooed hair waving nicely.

'Just bring ourselves,' Gwen says. 'And no, it's not in aid of anything except pleasure my dear. I like your pearls.'

'Thank you.'

'They're real?'

'Of course they're real.'

'Sorry.'

The taximan, a squat, dour fellow, whisked them there – Gwen just said 'Charlie Eliot's' – in less time than Penelope had to settle into the seat. And she was out again in a tree-lined street pressing down her dress, wondering did she get creases in the back from the seat of the taxi. She was about to ask Gwen to check but, remembering her lingering fingers the last time, thought better of it.

'This way,' Gwen says, having insisted on paying the fare. She pushes a button on a high steel gate. A grid opens. 'We're friends of Charlie,' Gwen delivers into the black rectangle. 'Invited.' The gate opens to a burly guy in a tuxedo blocking their way.

'And her?' the burly guy says nodding towards Penelope.

'My friend.' The man looks Penelope up and down (she could swear it's the shape of a gun she sees bulging through his tuxedo). 'Also invited,' Gwen adds. The man steps aside wordlessly to let them pass.

'Why did you say I was invited?' Penelope says.

'Trust me,' Gwen says.

Throbbing sounds of outdoor stereo music assail – hardly a complimentary word, she realises, but she wasn't really a disco girl – Penelope's hearing as they go through the scented garden. What is it, hibiscus or orange and exotic shrubs that she is unfamiliar with? The bougainvillaea showing off its great cluster

41

of purple flowers, she recognises, arraying the illumined white wall of the villa some hundred metres away. They hobble (Gwen gingerly on the gravel) towards that light through a winding path, flanked on either side by vegetation, jungle-like, and the image of the street without end in her writing enters her head as they pass by palms and cannas with their rubbery foliage and threatening giant cacti, and intermittently, recesses woven into the shrubbery.

'How big is this garden?' Penelope says.

'Big enough for a tryst. Eh, Pen?'

She called her Pen. She never called her Pen before; it was, she felt, forcing a familiarity not yet earned. Sheila called her that, and maybe Dermot the odd time; her father and mother, never, except once when she was small when her mother in her cups called her her little Penny. But normally it would be the full title. Indeed her father would have frowned at any abbreviation, of anything (and she newly wonders, why is abbreviation such a long word?). She feels Gwen's arm going through hers, tinkling little hairs like a simultaneous mix of shock and comfort, and the darkness of this jungle simulacrum to compound it all. Where is she going? What is she getting into? Who is this forward lady she is with? A few lampposts light their way, planted sparsely with their low lantern light.

The music grows louder as they draw nearer; she is able to recognise it now, Robbie Williams' *You're the One,* amid an increasing din of voices. How many people are at this party? Hundreds, lurking in all those hideaway places like a cackle of unfamiliar animals.

Gwen administers to Penelope's arm an excited squeeze, as a big heart-shaped pool unfolds itself before them.

A man is coming towards them. It's – Penelope draws a breath – Nails, the elderly guy from the beach with the pony tail.

Without saying a word, he plants a kiss hard and lingering,

like they are long-time lovers, on Gwen's lips. Gwen doesn't pull away, but sucks the kiss in with fervour; the look she gives, when eventually she unsticks her face, is one of gratitude. He is wearing a pink shirt with several buttons open to show off the now familiar Brillo pad of chest hair, and loose hanging linen shorts, doing nothing for his skinny legs and, as she looks down, good God, flipflops.

'How is my homegrown Gwenny baby?'

'Fine, Charlie. Charlie, I want you to meet Penelope.'

He takes Penelope's fingers into his square and gritty hand, and stooping down in mock chivalry, kisses them. 'Such long nails.'

He looks at Gwen. 'Where did you find this one?'

'She's my neighbour, actually.'

'Your neighbour?'

'Over here I mean, Charlie. She's a writer.'

'A writer,' he says scrutinising Penelope like a cartographer examining a map. 'And what does the writer write?'

'Novels,' says Penelope.

'Novels?'

The pause for further surveillance. He's undressing her, layer by layer; she can feel the garments fall. How long will it last, this ignominy? Oh, why did Gwen have to say that she was a novelist? What business is it of his?

'Good,' he says eventually and he claps his hands indicating the examination is over. 'Once you're not one of those journalist reporters.' He looks to Gwen. 'We don't need them spoiling our fun, do we, Gwenny baby?'

'No, Charlie.'

'They're not real writers, are they?'

'Charlie doesn't like the press,' Gwen says.

'Well, they're writers in their own way,' Penelope says.

43

'They're bolloxes,' Charlie says. 'They feed off the offal of others.'

'Come on, Charlie,' a group of girls are calling him from across the pool. He walks away but then looks back at Penelope.

'You got a knockout there, Gwenny baby,' he says. 'Get her to call to me sometime.'

'Did you hear his language?' Penelope says.

'It's just his way.'

'I wouldn't call to him if he paid me.'

'Anyway,' Gwen says dismissively, 'what'll we have?'

'I don't really know what to drink.' She's feeling uncomfortable. If she'd known for sure that the Lothario on the beach was Charlie Eliot, she would have thought twice about attending one of his parties.

'We have to have something,' Gwen says, 'to hold in our hand, as the actress said to the bishop.'

'All right, Gwen,' she says, 'I'll have a white wine.'

The bar is situated some yards in from the pool on a paved section in a smooth velvety lawn with dormant sprinklers at its side. It is a circular affair with little starlights studding its wooden ceiling topped with a conical roof of straw, just like the beach bar except more opulent, with the polished crystal and the greater array of drinks. The grey-sideburned barman, impeccably dressed in starched white, is doing tricks with cocktails, delighting a group of young women who go 'Ooh' and 'Ah' as he throws a glass in the air behind his back and catches it again. Penelope looks at the women, few of whom are English speaking (so much for Gwen and her expats); they are mainly blonde and eastern European, she would guess by their intonations. Some of them she recognises from the beach. They keep moving their bodies in rhythm to the music. It's an exhibition, a reverse of a peacock demo to attract the males – protuberant body parts, bumps and curves, vying to explode out of the taut tinder boxes of their skimpy attire. And she ponders, is this what Sheila wants, the copy she needs, the in-your-face thing that sells novels? And self-conscious now in that sea of unknown people, she would love to pick out Ramón somewhere, his reassuring kindly eyes. Gwen at the bar is swaying her ample hips exaggeratedly to the lively beat. The girls with the tight skirts – plain white or black – have given up on the bar tapping and are dancing now to the infectious strains of *It's Raining Men,* still holding their drinks: Piñas Coladas and Margaritas and Baccardi Breezers. Mixed couples are dancing up further at the end of the pool on a wooden decking near the DJ. The DJ is a guy with huge shades and shorn head who announces the songs with an English accent.

'He's the spit of Elton John,' Gwen says returning. 'Oh, I like that number. Shall we?' She places the drinks on a wrought iron table and takes Penelope's hand.

'People might get the wrong message,' Penelope says.

'What's the wrong message?' Gwen says.

'You know.'

'No, I don't know,' she says looking vexed.

'Sorry, Gwen, I didn't mean any...'

Gwen smiles. 'Forget it. Come on.'

On the dance floor they start swaying and gyrating in front of each other, Gwen trying too hard, Penelope not trying hard enough, to be cool and rhythmic, to go with the beat. Gwen, it seems to Penelope, is always one step out.

'It's been a while,' Penelope says.

'You'll pick it up.' Gwen says.

Penelope smiles, amused at the idea of Gwen thinking she is the expert. She looks around at the young, trendy women jarring with wizened perma-tanned males.

After the number has finished, Gwen takes herself off to the

Ladies and Penelope moves towards the pool, mingling with the crowd. She discerns a girl under the lamplight whom she recognises as the topless one from the beach, but this time of course in a dress – a tight puce number. That hussy, thinking she's being admired, flaunting herself under the light of the lantern.

Topless raises her hand to chew on a chicken wing. Penelope glances across the pool to the other side where there is a long trestle table with a white tablecloth and food, and, right enough, she can smell its varying odours now in the air, all sorts of fishy things and curry things on display, and rows of people milling around. Ice buckets, shining silver, and crystal punchbowls are being carried to the table by whitecoated waiters, and there is an explosion of champagne corks to high-pitched laughter. Topless licks her fingers. Her other hand rises from the lower darkness to slurp from a flute of champagne.

'How did you get on with lifeguard Ray?' she hears a tight black-skirted girl asking her.

'No further than a feel of his bleedin biceps,' Topless replies. 'I swear the bloke's a virgin.'

'Do you want to get some sweets then, Jane?' Black Skirt says.

'Why not?' replies Jane. 'We may have to wait a while for the snow.'

'You're going to do a line with Charlie?'

'Depends,' Jane says.

When Gwen returns with replenished drinks, they take up a position by palm trees not far from the bar.

'The food is up,' Penelope says.

'You hold those drinks,' Gwen says while I get us something to nibble.

'It's my turn to go,' Penelope says, but she takes the glasses nonetheless as Gwen smiles at her. 'I know my way about. We can't have you getting lost on us now, dear, can we?'

What is it with Gwen? Penelope wonders as she wanders off. She's flighty, edgy. Penelope looks at the lights around the pool strobing the people prancing about, imprinting on their clothes and faces and hands, transforming them into moving images, to the throbbing of the music, and she feels the decking itself pulsating.

Retreating from the noise, she hears voices behind her in the shrubbery and a rustling sound. She recognises Charlie's voice talking to someone. 'It better be good shit.'

She looks behind her. All she can make out is the silhouette of a man moving away through the trees, and that gatekeeper with the tuxedo, she can see hovering close. She watches Charlie walking along the path towards the villa, carrying a packet. As he comes into the opening, he sees Topless Jane washing down a 'sweet' with a gulp of champagne in the company of the girl in the black skirt. Charlie, without stopping, silently grabs Topless Jane by the arm and drags the unresisting girl with him through the dimly lit door of the villa.

Chapter Nine

She's down by the beach giving her head a chance to unwind, to unclutter the day's debris. She likes this time of night just before dawn when there is a cooling in the air, when she can breathe and think more easily. She walks along the wet firm part of the sand, just enough away to avoid the receding waves, in her loose cheese cloth gown, away from all that crowd of crazy people. Penelope had insisted on walking out, having had enough of Charlie Eliot's party. Gwen only made mild protest about leaving 'early', but had declined to go down to the beach with her afterwards; considered it daft at that hour, and went off to what she deemed her 'bye byes'. But Penelope knows the real reason was to avoid answering questions about Charlie, when she tried to prime Gwen about his drug-dealing. Questions like who, where and when? The people he dealt with? But Gwen was so evasive, so... almost defensive of him. 'Don't sound like the pigs' was all she conceded dismissively, sounding like some atavistic flower power protester, which is maybe what she is. But Penelope was glad to be shut of Gwen at that moment, to be shut of everyone, to be alone.

She sucks in the briny air, still feeling clammy from the party. Gwen had a point about the practicality of shedding a bra in such a hot climate. It is an encumbrance, a clinging thing. She walks away from the edge (she caught an unexpected splash), pushing her feet through the soft sand, past the empty recliners without their cushions now heaped up in rows resting from their sagging day. The cool night air embraces her as she makes her way out towards the hard sand once more following the tide out, tired of plodding through the high mounds of soft granulations which were straining her calf muscles. There is no one about. She sees a crab sidestepping at the water's edge, a sliver of moonlight lighting his way (where had the little pink fellow found refuge in the crowded daylight hours?). She experiences a feeling of oneness, with the crab, with the ocean, with the world as it was at the beginning, free from all the sweat marks of bodies that were stealing the sun just a few hours ago.

She listens. There is something on the wind. It is not just the ocean sound she hears. She listens intently, her jaw propped forward. It is the sound of oars, yes unmistakably, a boat, quietly sliding through the water, approaching. Unnerved, she retreats, half stumbling through the soft sand. She conceals herself behind a straw hut – the day time bar. She watches, her eyes wide in awe, as feet emerge from the waves, bare and silent.

Chapter Ten

The following morning it rains, an uncustomary outburst – it hadn't by all accounts rained for two months. Crowds of people huddle in the vestibule, those who were restricted to a week's holiday, particularly feeling hard done by, decrying their lot. They stand redundantly with their sea equipment: their snorkels and their bath towels and their already blown up Lilos, all their plans cancelled as they listen, trying to placate their whinging children. Why haven't they got a plan B? Penelope wonders. Weather is not a copper-fastened thing. Surely they should be prepared for such an eventuality. The weather has moods too, just like people, and now it's in a bad mood, a bit like her with her throbbing hangover headache.

Back in her apartment, she rests resignedly on her russet sofa bed – she had intended hitting the beach too; her stuff is just abandoned in a heap on the sofa: her pink bath towel together with her long-strapped canvas beach bag containing all her sea accoutrements, sunglasses in their case, various factor suntan lotions, books – two books only because of their weight – to peruse if the creative juices dry up, her black leather notebook, her three felt-tip pens, black for writing, red for editing and green, well, green for go, the pedagogic tick of approval, in their pine pencil case with its slide-on cover that she has kept since her schooldays, and which she always carries around with her even when, as is now, there is no script to edit. Not as yet. But there will be, and she can bring a few loose pages down with her to the beach whenever the story starts to evolve.

She looks out at the rain thundering down, striking at her balcony glass, streaming through gutters and gullies, having the temerity even to trickle in meandering rivulets onto her beige tiled floor. And she thought Ireland was the only aquatinted country, but Ireland's rain is only drizzle compared to this; this is the mother of all rains.

She rises from her chair; goes up to close tightly the balcony door, tut tuts at the flooded floor outside. Facing west, yes for the evening sun when it deigns to shine. She looks out at the rain seeping through that porous grey sky. How dark the world suddenly is. The rain, instead of easing, is getting heavier. It is after eleven now and, like heavy artillery, it is lashing into the swimming pool, and all around lakes are forming. How can a place flood so quickly? she wonders looking onto soaked dripping recliners, a deserted location which before one could hardly budge in, now appears like a ghost place except for the sound of muffled shrieks and the fading patter of feet of people caught out in the downpour. But those other feet, she ponders, in the darkness, were they of immigrants illegally sneaking into the county? Or the possibility of their being drug smugglers also could not be discounted. But one would have thought they would have chosen a more remote bay to disembark in than that of Felicidad. But maybe they were swept that way by the waves. And how thunderous those waves were last night, thinking of it now, harbingers of the storm today. But how many pairs of feet? she wonders, touched down on a new land? How many would make it, disappear into the underbellies of cities, personae non gratae? How many would be caught and deported, culling their numbers?

The rain continues to fall in great bucketloads. She writes for a while, works on the laptop looking out occasionally through the rain-studded glass of the closed balcony door on a dismal scene. Lightning flashes, exciting her, recharging her, and she pauses in her work waiting for – here it is – the thunder roll.

She eats her lunch in front of the small TV (to banish those interloping thoughts) which is perched on the teak sideboard of her living room. A baguette which she'd bought yesterday but still fresh enough, she had stuffed with tomatoes and cheese, and she sets it with a tumbler of water down on the low glass table. Just plain water. Today she couldn't stomach the glass of white wine which she would normally have with her lunch.

It's the quarter-final day of the women's singles at Wimbledon. Funny that, a dry day (but cloudy) over there. She looks only half interestedly at a Russian girl, tall and leggy, and she thinks of her fly-by-night neighbours next door. She hasn't heard a word from them. Well, she was too tired and tipsy anyway last night when she came back from the beach and just flopped into the bed. But this tall tennis player is grunting loudly at every shot (like sexual groaning), and is whipping her smaller victim, who is pumping sweat at a great rate, rendering her paraphernalia of wrist bands and head band inadequate, as she has frequent recourse to the towel. The smaller girl in time starts grunting too as she tries to recover, to get a toehold. Grunting is the name of the game. Penelope hates it; it's so unfeminine. Imagine if she had one of her characters doing such a thing in one of her novels, what would Sheila say? Is it just a habit? Forty love. She thinks of her brother with his child plastic trophies. Love means nothing in tennis.

Oh, she tuts, switching the TV off, that rain. She had hoped to work on the tan for the photographing session that Sheila promised would be forthcoming and... perhaps, who could tell? to catch a glimpse of Ramón again, standing high in his watchtower scanning the sea; or to marvel at his swimming (she had seen him) with the little lifebuoy trailing from him like a fish's tail, the graceful movement, the powerful arms like gentle oars powering him effortlessly, and at such pace. Oh, let him come. But does he fancy her? The way he came up to her, the way he spoke, those soft tones of his; but it's the eyes that tell the tale, rapt and concentrated as they were on her. But then, she sighs, did he not equally apply that same rapt attention to his volleyball? And Nails Charlie, hopefully she will avoid him, whatever is going on there. Talking about her as he did to Gwen (his Gwenny, his homegrown baby), as if Penelope were an object. Really! And Gwen apparently flattered by the lingering kiss or the pet appellations, not minding in the least. And yet she wants to know; she wants to find out. The periphery. I'm living on the periphery of things, she murmurs to herself, maybe not a totally bad thing for a writer, but, as she listens to the drumming of the rain, in these circumstances when one is not writing one likes to know where one is. And Ramón. Oh, how that Dermot had blocked him from her mind. But she would not let him anymore, no matter what; she would not let her brother resurrect the down thoughts; not now, not when she was at the point of gauging by Ramón's expressions and demeanour, what the Spaniard's intentions were towards her. Oh, she is sure if she met him again, and she imagines what it would be like, if she had one of her heroines rescued by him in a stormy sea. Oh, what had he said about her name? She thought back. Yes, she remembered, like Penelope Cruz. That was it, and the film he mentioned that was showing in the Centre. She could do worse on a rainy afternoon than go to the cinema. She recalls the name of the film: Volver: to return.

Chapter Eleven

People are splashing through the flooded pavements as she walks, panoplied ironically by her navy umbrella, which she had rather circumspectly brought with her from Ireland in case of eventualities. She'd asked Gwen if she'd like to come along. 'What?' said Gwen, 'to a Spanish film? You want me to go out in that downpour to see Vol what? No,' and her eyes lingered for a while, as if eyes could think; she would give it a skip.

The rain drips from the awnings of La Paloma Blanca as she passes by. How dull and cold it looks now, an erstwhile romantic place. Could romance itself be a false construct? Just a dressing on the raw reality of life. To live in a state of wishful thinking. And she remembers her plane being delayed coming in, and seeing a tall handsome stranger standing stoically in Arrivals (Llegadas) with flowers that had wilted from too long a wait. Surely not a thought for a romantic novelist to entertain. People are still in their shorts and T-shirts, and some even huddled in towels wrapped around damp swimming togs all caught out by the unpredictability of things. And so there they are, indulging themselves with early compensatory beers and wines and pizza slices as they look out forlornly from crowded cafés and bars on the flooded streets, some mumbling, trying to scapegoat the begetter of such a disaster. It's like a competition, an entertainment in itself to watch, to see which fleeing pedestrian will receive the most splashes from the passing cars. And, shrieking, they run, and people chatter and groan; some of them even find witticisms to make about the weather as if they were at home. And, as she walks, she sees the water finding its way, gurgling like a happy river along the street only to be thwarted by gullies and blocked shores. Sandbags have appeared – someone showing preparedness at least – at the door of the newsagent whose outdoor magazine racks, empty now, shake skeletally under the onslaught of wind and rain.

She must buy a newspaper. Yes, maybe after the film.

Shopping is always an option of course, she remarks to herself as she approaches the mall; her feet in her open sandals are wet, but she'll make do. Shopping – she never thought of it in such a context before – but it's like when one isolates something, like a single atom under a microscope (like something her father would do), you realise how intrinsic shopping is to the tourist package: when you take away the sea and the sand and the sangria, you're left with shopping, glaring at you. The shops are crowded; people perusing the stalls in plastic macs, engaging socially; people who, if the sun were shining, would not pass one another the time of day.

The cinema. One could walk past it despite its multiscreen boast (three screens actually) as it lies rectangular and flat-roofed, almost occluded between two restaurants, one of which is exuding pungent fish odours. She looks up at the posters, at the names of the other films advertised. A giant size Colin Farrell looms down on her with his dark smouldering eyes, ideal for a romantic novel, she considers (except for all those cigarettes he smokes); he could pass for a sheikh with eyes like that. Miami Vice. It would be rather fun to go in to see that film and hear his Dublin voice dubbed; it would give a different impression, a whiff of other cultures; what myriad nationalities will take away from a voice, and she will be familiar all the time with its subtle shades of meaning. You can't have too many argots, she notes mentally, when you're writing for a global market: they confuse the reader or the spectator and become lost in translation.

People in the foyer, all Spanish, young dating couples in the main, two guys holding hands. Well, so what? It's the twenty-first I'm-as-good-as-you century after all. Buckets of popcorn and litre-sized cartons of Coca Cola with long straws are all making their way into the cinema as if self-propelled. She pays for her ticket (she would've thought there would've been a bigger queue on a wet day like this, but the films are not in English, so cinema is not an option for a lot of tourists). It is more barato, more cheap, she knows the word, the girl at the ticket desk informs her, because she is going to the early show.

Some ads have started as she goes through the velvet curtains. She follows the torchlight of the usherette. The number of empty seats makes her choice of where to settle down difficult. A low-statured girl brushes past her, mounting the steps in a hurry to return to her friend whose 'pst, pst' sounds can be heard above. Blinded by her bucket (her bucket is her face, Penelope muses), she misses a step and falls, spilling the popcorn all down the aisle. The action detracts the usherette's attention from Penelope who continues to feel her way gingerly upwards, conscious of a sensation of being swallowed whole by the darkness – a transient fear again like her nameless lost girl had in the unknown street. But she must make a decision, and she opts for a middle row and exhales with relief on finding herself ensconced in the security of a double Pullman seat (are they all double, this binary thing again? she wonders). Still, to have space is nice, and she sinks into the wide plush cushion, lots of leg room; no one to her left, no one to her right; it's almost like a private showing, except of course for the low-statured girl with the spilled popcorn and, she has to admit, some hush hush 'callese' sounds from a couple of unseen quarters after the incident. But such vocal disapproval is shortlived, and even the usherette's torch is just a distant flicker now in the parterre. She looks at the screen. Those ads still blaring: a pretty darkhaired girl is putting her finger to her mouth slowly, sensuously (is that the way we eat? And she thinks of her wolfed-down pizza to get here on time). It is an ad for ice-cream – delicious, the sexual groan, the oral pleasure, the look on the girl's face staring into the camera wide-eyed (allowing the camera to take hold of her, to ravish her for the voyeuristic pleasure of us the viewers. So we can rush out and buy ice-cream, is that it?). Is that a reason why some rapes occur, Penelope wonders, and she pops a tic tac into her mouth. It's not always the fault of men; they are being conditioned, groomed by theses media gurus. Do they realise it? What can a girl expect from them, for God's sake, looking to stuff like this, being made to think that the generality of women are like that, this object of promised gratification on the screen? Yes, no matter what, she has to feel sorry for men. They will go out of this fantasy factory to inevitable disappointment with their testosterone levels charged, but they will find no outlet, unless of course there are more Topless Janes around to satisfy them. And those women of the night! Ah yes, of course: the law of demand and supply.

Still, she sighs, it is raining outside.

The film, what is the name of it again? Volver, yes, is starting. The credits are rolling. Pedro Almodóvar, the big name in Spanish cinema these days; she read about him, his fame as a director is spreading globally. All about his mother, was that the name of the other film of his she saw with subtitles in the IFI in Dublin? Seems to have a thing about mothers, and this one is about a mother returning from where...?

She soon learns it is from the dead that Penelope Cruz's screen mother returns. Ah here, she thinks realising, what have I let myself in for? What is Ramón sending her to see?

But the film begins to engross her, drawing her in to its pathos and humour. Penelope Eames keeps looking at Penelope Cruz every time she comes on screen, which is most of the time; she keeps scrutinising her rather than trying to concentrate on her words, to see if there is any resemblance of herself in her.

He, that is Ramón, said... but no, one moment, he did not say she was like her. He just remarked on the name being the same, that's all; everything else is speculation on her part. But he did recommend the film. How are people drawn to see certain films, she wonders, or to read certain books? It's all well... often, on hearsay. And off we go blindly on the word of others, and we find ourselves pronouncing on a work of art, thinking our ideas are our own, whereas if the truth be known, they have been unsuspectingly dripfed by others into our brains.

Which begs the question, she considers, as she pops another tic tac into her mouth, is there such a thing as a universally accepted work of art? Is it not all just a construct, a determination by an elite? Even Mozart, her father's favourite composer, she wonders, is it all propaganda churned out from the lofty towers of academe to dictate to hoi polloi what to think, to declare one artist better than another. To create a canon, a hierarchy. And what of Austen and Dickens, she wonders, the popular novelists of their day? When did the differentiation occur? When did the elite appear? When did a good story cease to be a good story? Chick lit to be looked down upon, her father had implied, he never actually came out and said it. No, because that would have left him open to argument, and possible contradiction. But to frown like that upon her, upon her literary efforts, his own flesh and blood, despising her, belittling her.

The people with the power and influence, they determine the aesthetic climate, and she thinks of the rain falling outside and, despite herself, feels warm and cosy in her Pullman seat, and can sympathise, as all writers should, with those caught out.

Journalists (who incur the wrath of Charlie Eliot) who may also be novelists, she thinks, returning to her artistic preoccupation, have an edge on mere novelists. In the manner, she has observed it, they are able to promote their own work in newspapers. And this review was written by... whose latest novel is entitled... Yes, plug your own tobacco. She was never asked to write a review of anything. Sheila never worked from that angle. How does one become a reviewer? She must ask Sheila next time they talk. Are chick lit/romantic novelists tolerated as reviewers?

And here now in this darkened room is Penelope Cruz with her fine figure, who doesn't really look like Penelope Eames (compare and contrast with the Special K girl). In height yes, but the Spaniard's hair is much darker, and she is thinner, less curvaceous than the writer.

And there is her mother now coming back from the dead, and no one batting an eyelid, as if the netherworld were some place just down the road, on her way to visit her family. Isn't that nice? Such a gesture, such thoughtfulness from one who should normally be busy at being dead. To come back like that, keeping in touch, some unfinished business, something left unsaid, like her own dead mother, and Penelope Eames thinks once more of her father, the man reduced, not dead but as good as, falling into the troughs of dementia, refusing to leave his Dundrum home, clinging to its walls like the old leech that he is. He prefers instead to sit at his window (on what once was his cathedra and is now his commode), and scowl at the world as if the world has done him an injustice, by failing to comprehend his greatness, by treating him as a mere mortal. He will not go with the tide of life. It is ironic, despite all his science, all his knowledge of tissues and anatomy, and experiments with stains and light and electrons and microscopy, he has failed to study the fundamental thing, which is of course how to prepare for your own extinction.

The nursing home in Booterstown which she offered to pay for (not that he needed the money) was a nice place by the sea; she had researched it: expensive but caring. 'I will not call for help until they coffin me.' Some old Gaelic poem she remembers he was fond of quoting about the last of the Irish aristocracy in the seventeenth century, resisting to the end the inexorable way of their country's history and their own eradication. Proud nobility or stubborn foolishness? I will not call for help until they coffin me. How such a phrase suited the cold defiance of her father.

But she ponders, sucking on her mint, could there be a possibility that he, like Cruz's mother who has now appeared on the screen, could return after he crosses that inevitable divide to discover the real wherewithal of things? That heaven will not be a place for his pontificating with an inexhaustible supply of obliging undergraduate females on tap. She pauses as if mentally taking breath. Yes, how like Charlie Eliot he is, but worse than Charlie in a way, because what he did was always done up to this in full compos mentis without the mitigating excuse of drugs; for he hated drugs, even alcohol or cigarettes he abhorred (her mother provided him with a field day for his ire in that area). Anything he felt that reduced the mind he opposed. He believed in the supremacy of his rational thought (failing to take cognisance that thoughts themselves can be slanted and thus also mind-reducing).

Could he return after he died? And her mother for that matter, who is already on the other side, if she were to return, what revelations would she have to unfold? Like Penelope Cruz's mother, returning to attend to unfinished business, or the business that drove her to the other side so prematurely. But as for him, old codger, that he would return in the guise perhaps of a penitent seeking forgiveness from his maligned daughter for all the years of prevention, of blocking – and she thinks of a computer term – of disabling her. Some hope of that, she accepts, that he would return with a big bag of confidence allsorts (she sucks hard on her mint) to bestow on her to enable her to go on;

not merely to go on but to prosper, to succeed, to make her feel wanted in the world and not – and that sinking fear strikes – as a mistake or aberration of birth. This professor, this man of science lacking in, and he did not even know it, humility.

Her mind, she summons back from its wanderings. She feels her half ticket as an assurance of her right to be here in this darkened room. She tries to concentrate on the words of the actors, which are too difficult for her to grasp fully. There is too much patois, but she gets the gist from the visual (why she sometimes reads comics in Spanish). The shades of difference, she's good at, the look, the gesture, all human life is the same, she concludes; body language tells it all.

Chapter Twelve

The sand in the morning is still too damp for bedless bathers to sunbathe on. She watches it for a while, those empty spaces, the caked mass slowly drying under a new sun, gradually disintegrating and returning to its fluffy powdery self. It is a noon sun that she sits under, the back of her sunbed pulled up as she browses through her newspaper which is in English. She feels she is cheating reading about Spain through secondary eyes, a special Costa del Sol organ for expats living in the environs. Lots of ads: Ears pierced while you wait (while you wait!), wife swop parties and things for sale on the same page. And the call girl services, mini pictures of girls with pouting lips and provocative poses (and of some well-endowed men too, flexing oily pectorals). All positions catered for, or so it would seem. And what position would she like? She never thought of it before. Lovers have positions? Love should dictate the position. A time guarantee, she reads, mere minutes for gratification.

Gwen is stretched on her front on a sunbed beside her, jellyquivering her buttocks, as she withers on like a broken record about being caught out. 'But I thought you weren't going to go out,' Penelope says. She had forgotten she needed bread and a few essential things. The rain had eased in the afternoon; she thought it was all over. But then the heavens opened again. A right soaking she got being caught out without her having even a plastic mac or umbrella, and she on her way from the Centre. Gwen sneezes suddenly. 'Oh dearie me.' The cruelty of the elemental world to upset her purchase of fresh croissants. 'I took three powders,' she is saying, and Penelope thinks, Beechams, how old-fashioned.

'Oh dear.'

'What?'

'I'm going to sneeze again.'

Is it an oxymoron, Penelope wonders, a sneeze under a Spanish sun? One would have thought she should have known, as Gwen reaches to return a crumpled tissue to the pocket of her small baby blue shoulder bag, after four years living in the county, to be prepared for such eventualities as a change in the weather. There is some excuse after all, Penelope has to grant, for the short-term package tourists; it's not in their brochures, such a thing. Gwen's voice seems to be gliding away from Penelope's consciousness as a sea breeze stirs up, and some other indecipherable voices can be heard. She sighs, as the waves crash. She looks towards Gwen who is engrossed in vigorously applying her Factor 3 to thin and rather veiny legs (in contrast to a thick upper and somewhat rotund middle). As for her ruddy complexion, which she appears to ignore, she would be better served applying a factor there.

She returns to her newspaper, checks the weather chart: Andalucía, twenty eight degrees. What is that in Fahrenheit? She always thinks in the higher numbers – to do perhaps with her longing for the enhancement of things? She tries to turn the page over to get to the front. It is hard to handle in this intermittent brine-laden breeze, making the paper taut and crispy like desiccated leaves.

Gwen grimaces as sand entraps itself somewhere between her hand and her lotion and her leg. Why do we only like some things from a distance? Penelope wonders, like sand in its smooth unruffled architecture; close up it's an irritation.

The paper crumples and blows out like a sail (if she's not careful she could be swept away). She steadies the page to catch the phrases as she reflects on the power of black ink to portray a world – a heavy responsibility for ink to bear. What if the writing were slanted like her paper is now? We depend on ink for the ring of truth. How do they pick headlines? To put something in, you have to leave something out. There is, there has to be, something happening in some part of this world which is of great importance and which is left out; it doesn't make the black; it is not recorded and therefore in the eyes of a great part of the world, such an event never happened.

Like her mother's death for instance; and she shudders despite the great heat. It was never recorded in the obituaries, on Father's instructions. Her mother didn't die. Her mother never existed. Connie Eames. Who heard of Connie Eames? And not even a tombstone to commemorate her; just – and she remembers – a cinerary urn from Mount Jerome crematorium. And even those ashes, their whereabouts, she does not know. Did her father scatter them from some mountain top to the four winds? And be done with her. She can hear his grumpy tones riding on that intermittent breeze.

Where then lies pity? Only in knowing can we feel for others? A death or a disaster in the infinity of disasters is occurring somewhere that we don't know about, that is unless someone decides to use the ink or the camera. She thinks of Dermot. Is there anyone recording what he is doing at this precise moment? Of course not. Is he alive then? Does he exist?

What are the headlines anyway? She shakes the crinkles from the paper. What's this, she wonders, her eye strobing down the page, another headline? LARGE QUANTITY OF COCAINE SEIZED. Where? Where does it say?

The sun is beginning to burn her. She applies the suncream, casts an eye towards Gwen, who is supine now dreaming of how she was caught out as she soaks up the sun. Should Penelope wake her? Is there a danger of her burning, that face unguarded, except for those sea shells planted in her eyes. But Gwen may not take kindly to being disturbed. She sighs and crumples the newspaper, greasy with suncream now, into her canvas bag. She squints out towards the windsurfers on the horizon. She will lie back for a while, soak up the sun too. Why not? She tries to push the upright of her sunbed down with her back, but it won't budge; it's supposed to go down just with the slightest movement of your spine; that's what you're paying for, after all, ease and comfort. It's stuck somehow. She scans the beach, but there is no sign of the boy who rents out the beds. Gwen snores; a fat lot of good she is. Penelope turns and fiddles with the rake-like teeth, strains, but they won't budge. Then just when she is at the point of... what? – swearing, giving up? she feels a hand against her shoulder. '¿Puedo?' May I? She knows the word.

His breath, his sweet breath, she is conscious of as he gently releases the gripping teeth, flattening the sunbed, smoothing it with his hand.

'You can lie back on it now,' he says.

'Lie back?'

'That was your intention, yes?'

'Oh yes.' She smiles. Those provocative glossy posers are being agitated into visibility in her bag by the breeze. Had he seen her poring over those pages? Maybe he thinks she is into such things. A slut? She banishes them hopefully by plunging them deeper into the entrails of her bag under her plastic water bottle and books.

And now, hands free, she regards her rescuer. Glistening droplets of sea water are meandering down his arms. Or is it sweat? She'd love to see him sweat, to behold the rugged, almost primal masculinity of him. Oh, so contrasting yes with what were the bony myopic exemplars that were her father and her brother. But those drops are of sweat, copiously showing that even he feels the heat newborn.

Oh, he is going away, having done his good deed; someone is

calling him, some of the volleyball players. She hadn't even heeded them, just a short distance from her, so carried away was she in her own little world.

'Wait,' she says, 'the film Volver ...'

'Ah yes.'

'You saw it? I mean down in the Centre?'

'I have seen it three times there.'

'Last Saturday?' she says.

'Last Saturday?'

'I went to see it.'

'Ah, the rainy day.'

'Yes.' Oh, what else can she say to detain him? 'It was a good film, moving.'

'Yes.'

Again the shout for Ramón.

'Un momento,' he shouts back.

The volleyball lands at his feet kicking up some of the newly dried sand. He picks up the ball, ignores the shouts of the volleyballers, and smilingly asks her, 'Would you like to play?'

'Me, to play volleyball? I haven't a clue how to play volleyball.'

'I will show you.'

He announces to the team 'Otra chica,' and the others smile and wait as Penelope rises and Gwen stirs in her dream. And he steadies her hand and shows her how to serve the ball. And the ball soars wide and out to the 'hard luck', the 'mala suerte' of team and onlookers (she hadn't realised she had created an audience for herself). There is no sign of Charlie Nails or his Russians or eastern European girls. There are Spanish girls here today. What day is it? Sunday, yes; they are free from work and are here to spend their day on the beach, dressed less provocatively than the other day players, Penelope notices, in ample bikinis, and not a monokini or thong in sight. The ball, her

66

second attempt rather weak, fails to clear the net, and he picks it up for her. Ramón closes Penelope's hand. 'Like this,' he says placing her fist under the ball and drawing her arm back, together they send it spinning over the net and the game is in motion. And soon she is diving in the sand with the best of them, one's vanities, one's feminine restraint, all out the window, as one would say. And dishevelled, she smiles at this new feeling in her, like the new sand drying and the new sun shining. The commotion wakens Gwen who sticks her head up from her bed and calls out, 'Penelope, in God's name what are you doing?' 'Come on and join us,' Penelope retorts. 'Not bloody likely,' Gwen says, but she is laughing nonetheless.

After the game (which her team won, to Penelope's delight. Her team! And with a star performance from Ramón), her serving hand is sore and red at the side. 'It is suave, your hand,' he says noticing, taking it into his. How tiny it looks immersed in his wide palm. 'Come with me,' he says. And he takes her to the beach bar, behind which she had hidden that night when she heard the sound on the waves. Ramón calls to Yambo, the black barman, for ice. And he rubs the ice cube on her hand, gently, softly, like a kiss.

Chapter Thirteen

He wants to see her tonight. They agreed to meet in La Paloma Blanca at eight; that is the time everyone meets, isn't it? 'That is if your hand is not too painful,' he added. And she remembers smiling at him for that: such thoughtfulness, such sensitivity. Could it have been simulated, such a caring attitude? she wondered (having read about the Don Juan culture in Spain). But it did not seem to be simulated. One can tell sincerity in a person's eyes, and his eyes were wide and unblinking, open yes, not trying to conceal. But her own eyes, she counters, beholding herself in the vanity mirror, are habitually downcast, shuttered, signifying a diffidence. What could one expect after all the years of procedure? What is one to make of eyes like that? Shifty, some people may say nesciently, but no, not shifty, just eyes that exude a lack of confidence (how do eyes do that? By their tremulousness, their hesitancy, their fear to engage one); inferior, humble, such qualities are to be read in her eyes which she has to admit in their own way are truthfully revelatory of what she is and was and always will be. Oh, and his touch, his hand on hers as he led her to the hut, healing the damages of years.

But now, what time is it? She glances at her watch: 5:25. She will have to get some work done. She has a goal now after all, an incentive, something really to look forward to (how long is it since?), unlike the spurious carrots she used to present as a spur to her writing in the past. If she got a chapter done, she would reward herself – depending on the mood and time of day – with a glass of wine or a cup of tea or a pyramid of Toblerone. Inconsequential things now, compared to this, the human carrot, the greatest incentive of all. Previously it was all so inner, all pertaining to her own little world, taking turns at being herself, but now... she really liked him. She talked all the way back to the

68

apartment with Gwen, surprising herself and indeed a tongue-tied Gwen with an uncustomary loquaciousness, as if she were usurping Gwen's own role. 'Did you see his eyes, so gorgeous and the competence of his touch?' 'Competence?' said Gwen. How he fixed her sunbed while Gwen slept. 'You were asleep?' 'Of course not. I heard every bloody word. A load of tosh.' And Penelope, regardless, continued breathlessly recounting how he eased the pain in her hand after the volleyball game. 'I knew you shouldn't have played that,' Gwen said, continuing in her deprecating tone. 'Oh, but he was so gentle, Gwen,' 'Ha.' Talk of Ramón seemed to have worsened Gwen's condition. 'A summer cold, maddening in't it?' she said as she pressed the button for the lift, and it was two, not one mosquito bites that were tormenting her now. Her legs were swollen. Would she need antibiotics? she wondered. She is going to purchase a net; she had sworn before, she would get a mosquito net to cover her entire bed. But she was happy for Penelope, she said in a self-sacrificing tone. 'Go out and enjoy. Don't mind me.' She would lie down and would see Penelope in the morning. 'Hopefully,' she added as if to say her suffering was so bad she might not survive till the next day.

Chapter Fourteen

She checks her mobile messages. One from Sheila enquiring about the progress of her tan. The press photographer from *The Female on Sunday* will be in Spain next week with journalist Tiffany Pringle to interview her on her change of abode, and how she's finding her adopted country and how it affects her modus operandi and what her plans are now and... she will provide them with a sneak preview perhaps of her next book etc. etc. And thus the forewarning tone from Sheila, she had better be ready.

She writes quickly with her black felt-tip pen on loose sheets of A 4 paper, her racing mind driving the words into an almost illegibility. Not too much at a stretch; a few hundred words would do or she would not be able to read back what she had scrawled, to type into her laptop. That girl, she has not even assigned a name to her as yet, no more than the street she eventually wound her way out of, or even the city of which it was a part; but they will come, those elusive spectres from her subconscious; they always come in the end or in the middle or even towards the end of the beginning. These things wade through the slush waters of the unknown mind. Be welcoming, she enjoins; when they knock, let them in. To create, to write is an open doors activity:

The girl has escaped the city and is walking, in contrast now, in the countryside. By fields she makes her way...

What is that sound? Penelope wonders rising. She goes to her balcony railing, looks down. It's coming from the pool as she had figured: the din, from posturing adolescents. If she were renting now she could complain and possibly change to a quieter apartment, but she has purchased and is therefore stuck with this. She sighs and closes the sliding door which at least muffles the sound.

70

Returning to her glass-top table which she had brought indoors when the rains had started, Penelope sits in shadow, the sunrays fading outside. Her pen scratches on a new white sheet:

By fields she makes her way on a quiet boreen. The fields are warm and golden with sunflowers turning to greet her as she passes by, and vineyards in the next field laden with their promise of Bacchanalian nights. Oh, the night is looming. Is there a charge in the sky? An evening star twinkles down on her as she walks in her flowing primrose summer dress, from which lithe tanned legs step out as she advances, and up further now she can make out peasants, as in a distant painting, working in the fields, their faces shaded by their straw hats, and they are dressed in sable colours. Why the dark colours, she wonders, in this happy golden land? They smile as she draws nearer, toothgapped smiles of old people wizened from a life of hard physical toil, who in time, she surmises, will sink stoically back into the earth, from where they had come, from where we all have come. But not to dust, not that, that terminal word; more than that surely, a return to a harmony, that is the word, with the earth, with... and she looks up at the chrome blue sky... with the universe. She negotiates a smooth bend in the road adding to the mystery of her journey. After a while the fields empty and she is in a land poor and arid. And in the heat-hazed distance some yards in from the road she sees a dead leafless tree. She cannot name it by its branches; and so there is a branch, a person, a place all nameless. The tree is sinewy, contorted and, as she looks closer, with a blue rope hanging into the shape of a noose with nothing at the end of it.

Is that what she felt, her mother, she wonders, that there was nothing at the end? Affrighted, Penelope puts her pen down. Her mother. It was alcoholism she died from, the liver giving out, cirrhosis, what her father had told her more than once was the cause of her death (sparing nothing in his technical jargon: ...'the death of cells producing interlacing strands of fibrous tissue behind which are nodules' etc.). But Penelope, suddenly realising, never saw her mother die. She only saw her dead, the white shroud covering her up to her chin before the coffin lid came down. Penelope had been away. She'd won a prize for a story – a week in London, all expenses paid. It was seven years ago, yes. Dermot had just finished secondary school, and so glum and sullen he was rather than mournful when she returned; she couldn't get a word out of him for months afterwards. And that's the way it is perhaps, the different reactions of a brother and sister (she wanting to talk and talk) to a mother's death. Yes, that eleventh-hour telegram from her father – 'Your mother has finally succumbed'. It was done. Everything left, she remembers, in what he deemed, in a rare human compliment, the capable hands of cosmetic beauticians. Oh, but he could have contacted her sooner – she could have cut short her trip, instead of tarrying as she did over London's sights. And he never condescended – not once in his life despite her giving him the number – to communicate with her on her mobile phone. Yes, that alcoholism, so slow (and so fast in the end), an almost socially acceptable form of death. And she looks down at the black ink, barely revealing, in that dreamy scribbled hand.

She sees him standing, waiting for her outside la Paloma Blanca. Leaning against one of the restaurant's two mock Doric pillars in a white open-necked shirt and chinos – are they black or charcoal? She can't quite make them out in the darkening evening? And shining black leather shoes – did he polish them specially for her? And his gelled hair combed back enhancing his high brow; a high brow – and she thinks of her father briefly and his prominent forehead: an intellectual, a clever boy, it can go with the physical; there is no law other than cliché that says they should be dichotomous. He's looking down the street, the opposite direction from which she is approaching. Come to think of it now, she did not tell him the name of her apartment complex: Playa de Mar. She just called it – how silly – her apartment. But he is staring (with his right leg raised now against the pillar) bemusedly, it seems to her, at the tourists as in their droves they strut and swagger along the street stalling at stalls and popping in and out of shops haggling over jewellery or swimsuits or leather purses, forcing sun-engorged feet into tight bargain shoes. And all such activities are engaged in on the footpath; the stall owners make a premium of the public thoroughfares, forcing passersby onto the road to the hooting of irate motorists.

'Hola,' she says touching his right elbow.

'Hola. You look very... nice,' he says eventually as if lost for the word.

He has already booked a table for two upstairs in the roofless part of the restaurant. The evening is warm enough, but she had brought her white pashmina shawl on her arm anyway (she must buy a bolero and look more the part). A table in a corner with a sea view. So much more upmarket, like a different restaurant in

73

contrast to the more hands-on functionality of downstairs where she had dined the first night.

'Is it okay?' he says, holding the seat for her.

'Lovely,' she says.

'Lovely,' he mimics.

'What?'

'The way you say it.'

What way did she say it? What did he mean?

A white candle flickers beside a solitary red rose, long-stemmed, still partly in bud, she notices, promising things, as it peeps up from a narrow ceramic vase. The same smiling waiter she had met the first night. 'Ah, la señorita. Tonight you have company,' he says, presenting the menu.

'You know each other?' Ramón says.

'I dined here before.'

'I see,' he says. 'So how was your day?'

'My day! Oh good. Well...' she thinks of her writing efforts, '... not bad.'

'Not bad?'

'Not bad. Again not an enquiry but a repetition as if he is learning her language, as if he is trying to speak with her accent to commune with her, she would like to think, all the more closely.

He smiles, his dark eyes flashing in the candlelight.

'And what did you do with your day,' he is saying, 'that was not bad?'

'I'm trying to write a novel, actually.'

'Ah, you are a writer.'

'Does that sound terribly boring?' And she thinks alarmingly, would he respond like Charlie did in his outburst on the nature of journalists?

'Not at all. What is this novel about?'

74

'It's meant to be a romance like my first novel. That's what they want.'

'They?'

'My publisher, my agent.' She sighs. 'My readers, I suppose.'

'You sound like you're apologising.'

'Do I really?'

'When you say what they want. What do you want?'

'What do I want?'

'Yes.'

She sighs once more, longing for that cigarette in her handbag. She wasn't expecting an interrogation, benign though it may be.

'I don't know exactly,' she says reaching for an olive from a bowl which a waiter has placed on their table in passing.

'Ah, but you are already published,' he says

'The way it is,' she says, finishing the olive (what will she do with the stone?), 'you're judged on your second work, which I'm afraid is presenting problems.'

'Ah, yes.'

'Like this character, the young woman I am writing about, she is lost.'

'Lost? Where?'

'Everywhere.' Self-consciously she removes the stone from her mouth and places it back in the bowl and, surprising herself, compulsively reaches for another olive.

He smiles. 'You like the olives,' he says pushing the bowl nearer to her.

'No, no, I've had enough really,' she says, fearing he will think her a glutton. 'She keeps getting lost,' she says, 'every time I write about her. She keeps running away. I can't catch her. In the streets of a city, in country boreens.'

'Boreens?'

75

'Little country roads.'

'I see.'

The waiter arrives. Starters. She chooses the melon; he chooses the onion soup.

'And your main course, are you ready?'

'Conejo,' she says. Rabbit, yes she knows the word. 'I never tried it. People went off the rabbit ever since the myxomatosis scare years ago. My mother used to tell me about it back home in Dublin.'

'Ah Dublin,' he says, 'that's where you're from.'

'You've been there?'

'Many times.' He smiles. 'I studied English in Dublin for many summers. My mother, she used to send me there, to visit what she called my ancestors.'

'Your ancestors? What is your surname?'

'My appellido is O'Donnell-Lorca.'

'O'Donnell-Lorca,' she says incredulously.

'El conejo y la pasta,' he says to the waiter who is standing uncomprehendingly with his smiling face.

'And wine?'

'You choose,' she says to him.

He picks a rioja tinta from the wine list.

Handing back the menu to the waiter, he folds his arms and looks straight at her.

She gives a little shiver. Is it to break his stare, or involuntarily due to the sudden gust of wind coming up, flickering their candle?

'Your chal,' he says

'My chal? Oh, my shawl,' she realises as he points.

'Perhaps you should...'

'Perhaps I shall.'

'Allow me.'

He rises and drapes the pashmina over her shoulders. So gently; was a shawl ever so light before, like eiderdown?

'But you...' she says, banishing a blush and steeling herself to look at him as he resumes his seat, as if a different person is sitting before her now... 'you're part Irish then?'

'Perhaps,' he says.

'Oh, you may be one of the Wild Geese,' she exclaims excitedly, remembering from her history the Flight of the Earls in the seventeenth century, signalling the end of Irish aristocracy. And she thinks of that poem of defiance her father had, decrying their loss.

'Are you familiar with Madrid?' he says.

'No.'

'There is a street there named Calle de O'Donnell.'

'Oh, named after Hugh O'Donnell, the great earl.'

'No, I don't think so. It may be his descendant perhaps but the street is called after Leopoldo. He was a governor who set up a constitution in the nineteenth century. But I think he was born in Tenerife, so... I can't say for sure if he is my ancestor. He was poisoned, I think.'

'Ah.'

She is disappointed, not so much for his poisoning, but for a moment she thought she was entering the annals of history by dating the descendant of an Irish earl.

'Still,' he says, noticing the disappointment on her face, 'it is possible; there are so few O'Donnells in Spain.'

'And so many in Ireland. It would be interesting to follow it up.'

'Perhaps. But does it really matter, things like that?' His tone is earnest now. 'What difference would it make to me now as I sit here? The dead, you can't go back that far; they've no meaning; they don't touch you; they're just artefacts.'

'Your English,' she says, 'is fluent.'

'Maybe,' he says, 'it is when I talk on these things there is a similarity in the languages. Abstract things, not words like shawl, but concepts, they tend to adopt a lingua franca, don't you think?'

'I'm afraid I don't know enough of your language to comment.'

'But,' and his brow wrinkles, 'parents, grandparents perhaps, that's about all we can hope for.'

'Hope for?'

'To commune with. You see the premise to go back further is false; it presumes that in going back that far, centuries say, we should somehow be like them. But such a thing is impossible.'

'You're not out to impress then,' she says, not knowing whether to compliment or censure him.

'What would be the point of that?' he says.

What is she to make of him? On the one hand he appears so romantic, but here talking about death and ancestors, he seems almost... cynical.

She sighs.

'You look triste.'

'Sad.'

'Triste is a better word.'

'No, I'm fine really.'

'This young woman who is lost,' he says, 'tell me about her.'

'Maybe later, when I have written more, I will be able to tell you then.'

'I can wait.'

'But you,' she says, surprising herself by her boldness in holding his stare now across the flickering candle, 'why did you ask me out?' But she can't keep it up and her own eyes are cast down now not in shame but rather – and her eyelashes are fluttering – in coquettishness despite herself.

'Why?'

'That film, remember?'

'Volver.'

'Yes.'

The sound of a cork popping. The waiter with the wine.

'You taste it,' Ramón says.

The waiter pours. She lifts the glass, tastes. 'Estupendo.'

'You remember Penelope Cruz,' Ramón says as the waiter departs. 'She sang a song in the film, a song from childhood that her mother had taught her.'

'Yes, it was very moving.'

'Well, you are the echo of that song.'

She laughs. 'Echo! Is that all I am, an echo?'

He touches her hand across the table. She feels a tingling sensation travelling all the way up her arm, all the way to her trembling heart. She disengages her hand from his shyly with the excuse of sipping her wine. But the rabbit, pungent in its juices, fills her with daring. The wine is strong, the hand was gentle and he is saying these things. This is it at last, this is the romance, the stories, all those holiday love trysts, in the garish paperbacks that clutter the airports and summer beaches of the world, what Sheila wants, what everyone wants her to deliver, this is it; she is the echo of that song.

'The echo that sings to my heart,' he is saying, 'when I saw you on the beach it is of my madre, you understand, my mother.'

'Your mother?'

'Yes. You remind me of her.'

What? she wonders. She is crestfallen; not Penelope Cruz but the old dear in the film. Oh, surely not her.

'When she was young,' he says as if reading her thoughts.

'Ah.'

He touches the tips of her fingers. She doesn't draw away.

'My mother returns to me.'

'How do you mean, returns to you?'

'From the dead?'

'From the dead?'

'Yes. She passed away when she and I were not ready. So when someone leaves like that, unexpectedly you understand, they have to return. It was when I went to that film I understood.'

Is he for real? She does not know what to think. He is so serious for a guy on a first date, for any date. Does he expect her to sit rapt and believe all this? But there is such a sincerity in his dewy eyes. And the deep tremulousness in his voice, like a romantic poet (or what she imagined a romantic poet to be), and yet robust with the rough century jarring in him now and again. But to talk of death!

The smiling waiter is standing at the table holding the braid-tasselled menus.

'Postre.'

'What would you like?'

'Nada,' she says. 'Estoy... llena.'

'Qué bueno,' the waiter says. He has shining white teeth, or is it just the candlelight that is making everything appear shiny. She looks out at the lights twinkling on the yachts down in the marina and the moonlight gilding eddies so bright, turning to silver Ramón's white shirt. There is a distant hum of a guitar and the heady scent of jasmine wafting on the air. She looks around. Yes, the adjoining tables are free, and she feels it, loose, chatty, like the way she was with Gwen a while ago with a new-found tongue. And she is even competing with Ramón now for the lion's share of the wine-mellowed words.

'Your Spanish is good,' Ramón says.

'Basic,' she says. 'Not good enough to follow all of that film.'

'You understand,' he says placing his fork down, 'the concept of eternal return?'

'What?'

'People,' he says, 'never really go away. The ones near to you I mean. You are weighted by them. Pesado. You can say?'

'Weighted, yes.' Weighted. What a word.

'The act of birth itself is a product of weight.'

'I'm sorry. I don't understand you, Ramón.'

She feels her neck; it feels bare without the pearls.

'Perhaps,' he says looking at her quizzically, 'it is I who bore you.'

'Oh no.' She dwells on the unintended pun on birth in the context of what they are saying – things can be hilarious in the mixup of languages; could cause an international furore if it were on a political stage. And she muses: emotions can be mixed up too; got to be careful there. 'Please continue what you were saying.'

'Well, you know the woman lies under the weight of the man...'

Not always, she was going to blurt, but she was too shy to say it, and she thinks of those advertised sexual positions in the magazine which she was trying to conceal from him earlier.

'When they are making love. Yes?'

'I suppose.'

'No,' he says, 'not suppose. Out of the weight comes the birth. The bambino grows and carries his own weight.'

'What has that got to do with eternal return?'

'Love and birth.'

'Love and birth?'

'When my mother gave birth to me.'

'You have a very old wisdom,' Penelope says, 'for someone so young.'

'I don't know. Perhaps. But what you say about me, it is because I think a lot.' He smiles pointing to his forehead. 'Can you see the... how you say, the...?'

'Wrinkles. No,' she says. 'And you are also the great lifeguard.' She should have said a lifeguard realising too late the possible sarcasm in the definite article. And for a bizarre moment she thinks of her father's incongruous fondness for the film star Victor Mature, something she could never understand. That adulated alpha male of his time playing Samson was one of her father's favourite actors; (but he couldn't act, she could not tell him that). He kept that old video cassette of Samson and Delilah.

'Not great,' he says, 'okay.'

'But...' She steals an under-eye glance at his biceps, curtails a desire to actually feel them (what Topless Jane had surrendered to; but she will not succumb that easily), and the deep cavity of his chest making his shirt, as he breathes, billow like a welcoming tent. And her father is now the he-man. At least that must have been his desired self-image with his skinny physique camouflaged by the ballooning academic robes. He would play that relic of a cassette at least once a year, reinventing himself as Victor Mature, while fondling those female ready-to-please undergraduates on his flight of fancy. He was the one turning that grinding stone, his muscles tautening from the great striving of human, no masculine (a slip, Penelope, but all is forgiven) endeavour to reach a climax. Oh yes, Victor Mature.

'A coñac,' he says, noticing her empty glass, 'to finish off?'

'But what I was saying...' he says as they walk under a waxing moon towards her apartment.

'Sorry, I interrupted you.'

'No no.'

Sorry. How easy it to say sorry to someone in different

82

contexts.

'It's okay.'

She laughs. She can no longer constrain herself. What's possessing her to laugh like this? Is it the wine and that coñac combining to create this uninhibited outburst with her head thrown back and her hair undulating. It's like she's laughing at her father, and this young man is the catalyst... it is preposterous.

'I'm sorry. I'm not laughing at you, Of course not.'

He throws her a puzzled look.

'It's just I'm... well, happy or perhaps merry is the word. But please continue.' She links him. God, she is tipsy being forward like that.

He smiles, reassured.

'Please continue.'

'Well,' he says, 'what I believe is that if there is love at conception there will always be...'

She titters. 'Sorry. Please go on.'

'You want me to go on?'

'Oh yes. Please forgive me.'

'All right,' he says. 'Well, the way I see it is...' (and a slight nervousness has entered his voce)... 'if there is love, there is memory, because we remember the things we love more than the things we hate.'

'Is that true? I wonder.'

'Yes, it's a universal thing. Freud tells us.'

'You've read Freud?'

'Of course. He shows that we banish the things or even deny the things that cause us pain. And love is the eternal in us.'

'But what do you mean by return?'

'My mother, she returns every time I remember her.'

'Do you believe in ghosts, Ramón?'

'Now,' he says, 'I am boring you.'

'No. Not in the least.'
'No?'
'No.'
He smiles.

Chapter Sixteen

She is in that field where she sees a stone, and she is drawn towards the stone like someone hypnotised. It is the size of a book. She lifts up the stone; it yields easily, revealing the dark underneath and little creatures scurrying away from the light.

And the real life thoughts interrupting. Oh, Ramón, he is so sincere, so serious. She thought – she had hoped – he might have kissed her (it wouldn't have killed him), at her apartment complex, before bidding her good night. But then she never invited him in. He could've got a message of dismissal; the bashful first date, the weighty talk. Was she bored with him? The way she had laughed at him. Did he take offence? She was only trying to introduce a little levity – such uncustomary temerity she knows was wine-infused. But a note of uncertainty was left hanging in the warm night air, despite all the earlier mutual politeness and eye-gazing.

The effects of the wine and the coñac have worn off, and now after two mugs of strong tea, she is as sober as a judge – oh, not a judge. Watch the clichés, Sheila always said. Sober as what then? As nothing, just sober; sober now. But it is like there is something impatient in her to allow indulgence in intoxicated reverie, something willing her on. She must grasp that feeling; never let such a drive escape, whatever the time – and she glances at her watch: 3:25. Tap tapping on the laptop, trying to decipher some of her late night scribbles. Gwen will be calling in a few hours to catch the early morning beach; she knows that, but in the meantime she must... she must write. She thinks of her youth, images her father and herself: the stern lean meat of him always looking down as from a great height like one of those high statues in O'Connell Street of great men. Looking down on a bemused pigtailed girl, a strange object beneath him, an obstacle which he would have willingly trodden on or kicked out of his way in his forward scientific advance. And she, the little girl, not quite cowering but wondering, always wondering what she could have done to make her daddy like her; to find some way of reminding him that he was her daddy. Even to engender a little freckled smile perhaps in the hope of his frowning less.

In his eyes why was she such a disappointment to him? It's a new angle to adopt, trying to be objective, seeing through the eyes of the enemy. Is it possible though, she wonders, to be objective about such intimate matters? With the help of Ramón perhaps. She feels so safe with him; would love to confide in him. She really likes him; the very quirkiness of the way he looks at the world she finds endearing. And so searingly honest. There would be no chicanery between them. His simple equation of love and weightedness. But is it really possible to undo all that went before, all that paternal drilling?

She lies down on the bed, hugging her pillow. Her eyes are tired and itchy but she resists rubbing them for fear of making them sore and rheumy. She sees the dawn light appearing at her balcony, but that stubborn moon is staying put in the brightening sky. Love replaces hatred; it couldn't be simpler; just a quick substitution. But how could she love her father or Charlie Eliot or a one such as Topless Jane even? It was asking too much.

Chapter Seventeen

'I just want to pop into the nail bar before we go down,' Gwen says. She is standing at Penelope's front door, holding her shoulder bag and dressed in a loose-fitting wisteria-blue frock. 'Don't worry, my swimsuit is underneath,' she says, just in case you think I was forgetting. I broke a nail,' she says. 'You won't believe how.'

'How?' Penelope sighs.

'Closing a cupboard door in my kitchen; it just caught and broke in the hinge. See.' She holds up her right forefinger for Penelope to examine the split in the plate of the nail reaching down to the lunula. 'I can't go to the beach like this. It would get caught in everything.'

'Can't you just cut it?' Penelope says.

'Cut it?'

'Duh!' Penelope says. 'Like with a scissors?'

'Good God no.'

'Or you could let Charlie chew it for you,' Penelope continues, surprising herself with the delight she is taking in teasing Gwen.

'Charlie wouldn't be interested in me.'

'Why not?'

'Not pretty enough for him I'm afraid. But let's get a move on,' Gwen says. 'I need to get my other nails done anyway. The varnish is fading. See.' And she proffers her nails again for confirmation. 'I promise you, it won't take long. Besides, you might be interested in this too.'

'In what precisely?' Penelope says.

She takes Penelope's hand in hers to examine it. 'Getting your nails done, ducky.'

'My nails are fine,' says Penelope, pulling her hand back.

'Oh, I know what it is,' Gwen says, 'you can't wait to meet

87

your Raymond.'

'His name is Ramón.'

'Touché,' Gwen says, her voice rising a pitch. 'Anyway the thing is, Pen,' and she links her with her left arm drawing her out the door, 'you can tell me all about your beau as we go. Oh,' and she giggles, 'that rhymes.'

It also shows your age, thinks Penelope. Who uses the word beau nowadays?

They walk down to the shopping mall, Gwen holding on to Penelope, for fear she will run away perhaps down to the beach like a lovesick heroine. 'It's just down a bit,' Gwen is saying with her singsong cheerfulness, forcing Penelope to step out smartly to keep up with her. Colin Farrell, Penelope notes, as they pass by the cinema, is no longer on the bill, but Volver with a giant picture of Penelope Cruz is still showing. Is it true what the newspaper said in the review of the film, that Cruz had to have buttock enhancement for her part? Oh dear, if that is so, thinks Penelope Eames, eyeing the mournful Cruz, what they do for film, and those crocodile tears – and this is the strange bit – provoking real tears, a real tristeza in Ramón and indeed in her as well.

'Stop dawdling,' Gwen says pulling her away. (She is behaving like an overbearing aunt whom Penelope is beginning to resent). 'Really Pen, what's possessing you to ogle those foreign films? Double Dutch, that's all they are. You'd think they'd have a few decent films in the King's English.'

They ascend a wooden stairway behind the cinema until they come to a green door with Paraiso de las Uñas engraved in gold on it, and underneath manually scribbled in black felt-tip: Nail bar now open. Just Nail bar, thinks Penelope, something's lost in translation.

'You see,' says Gwen, 'at least it's in English: Nails. Have a look at the list. Is there anything you'd fancy?'

On a big white placard in Spanish with English subtitles, Penelope reads:

Nail extensions, gel or acrylic €60
Refill   €35
Manicure €20
French Polish   €12
Spray tan   €35
Gel on toenails   €40

'You should get that done,' says Gwen.

'What exactly?' says Penelope.

'Gel on toenails. That's lovely.'

In the Paradise of Nails the Spanish girl assistants are murmuring about the drug haul, the odd word leaking into Penelope's comprehension – drogas... policía. There is an air of nervousness about the place as the assistants throw furtive looks towards the door every time the lintel bell tinkles. Who are they expecting?

While they are waiting to be called, sitting on a rather sticky plastic-covered bench, the headlines that Penelope had read about stare at her in Spanish from a tabloid newspaper splayed beside them.

'You heard about the drugs seizure?' Penelope says.

'Not the first time,' Gwen says concentrating on her broken nail.

'Could it be Charlie's?'

'Charlie's? What makes you say it would be Charlie's?'

'You have a soft spot for him, don't you, Gwen?'

'The thing is I know Charlie of old.'

'Of old?' Penelope says

'Yeah. He's from Spitalfields too you know.'

'No, I didn't know,' Penelope says. 'I didn't even know you were from there.'

'Well now you do,' she says. 'Everybody picks on poor old Charlie. Anything that happens in this place, Charlie is blamed. They should investigate some of their own, those Fascist pigs.'

Chapter Eighteen

The heat is intense. She kicks the sheet off her. And it is only what? She checks her bedside clock, hardly nine o'clock. She rises and opens the balcony door fully, and goes to the front door and leaves it ajar, catching it with a chair. At least that should provide a little welcome draught. There is nobody about this early, so it should be safe enough. Sleep has won out with those late night revellers, till when? Till near noon when the patter will be heard once more and choruses with their myriad possibilities to subsume the tranquillity. Only then will it be time to close the door.

She must purchase a fan, yes; it would have cost a lot extra to have had air conditioning installed, more than she had to spare at the time, keeping as she was a little reserve in the event of her father ultimately consenting to go into a nursing home. And she saw neat electric fans on their own stand, quite inexpensive, down in the supermarket.

And now she sits in her pyjama bottoms on the dralon stool at the vanity mirror to do her daily breast check. Just a few minutes a day could help save your life, the nurse told her. She remembers the five point awareness code:

Know what is normal for you. The normal size, yes, firm, unlike the hanging walls of Babylon as they are on some women (Gwen for example). But then there is Topless Jane to account for, going around with nothing at all to show, like men and their nipples; she chuckles, funny creatures.

Look and feel. She looks more closely into the oval-shaped mirror, the scar healing, disappearing as if there had been nothing there at all, after that operation she had arranged alone. Her father, how could she have told him, or Dermot? She told Sheila of course and half regretted it with all her talk about input and output; she just let it slip; she can be quite insensitive, can Sheila. Concentrate now.

Know what changes to look for. The sides: no trace of lumps.

Report any changes without delay. Nothing to report.

Attend breast screening if fifty or over. Doesn't apply. Armpits, or arms, all normal. No discomfort, just that little strip of sunburn that slyly seared the top of her left breast, that day when she lingered under the pre-noon sun; she was careless then. She reaches for her Aftersun. Gently massages. The nipple: no discharge, no bleeding, no rash. No dimpling, denting or scaling, she remember the words used by Nurse Slattery, or discoloration of the skin, or nipple inversion – yes, she remembers her saying that. The right nipple now she works on, conscious of the erection staring out at her, telling her she is normal, confirming her as a sexual being.

A sound, a slight movement behind her. She looks up higher in the mirror and sits back startled: another image has appeared. The face of Gwen silent, staring.

'The door was open,' she says.

How long was she there staring? Could she not have knocked? It would have been the polite thing to do, whether the door was open or not. And she covers herself with her arms as if only now aware of her nakedness.

The touch of Gwen's hand on her shoulder, the lightness of that touch, and she thinks for a moment of Ramón, and the touch sends a not unpleasant shiver down her spine. Succumb, succumb, the touch is saying to those great enfolding breasts, the swale of which Penelope can make out in the mirror from Gwen's low buttoned blouse. Oh, to ensconce oneself in there, to suffocate or perhaps to dream, to go back. Yes, she is like a mother in a way, Gwen, but not her mother, who was always in a state of bother. Gwen is calm, confident. She must be what? at least ten years older than Penelope, and is not without her irritations: her bossiness for one thing, steering her clear of the cinema like that when Penelope wanted to linger and look at the posters; and her philistinism: the second painting which she purchased for Penelope was even more tacky than the first, featuring galloping ponies. Why in God's name would she want to watch galloping ponies in an anonymous setting all day long? What inspiration would these bland imitations by second rate artists provide? 'That will cover the space nicely for you,' Gwen had said with self-satisfaction, holding the picture up to the unfaded square of paint. And thirdly, her gross ignorance of the country in which she resides.

But she is bare despite the awkwardness of her arm covering, and in the mirror the hand, Gwen's hand resting still on her shoulder, refuses to go away.

'I... left the door ajar for the air to circulate,' Penelope says to break the telling silence. 'It is stifling. Do you not find it stifling?'

'Yes.'

Penelope is conscious of the globes of sweat forming on her forehead and her arms, her underarms especially, they are embarrassingly seeping, but Gwen keeps smiling into the mirror.

'You look quite beautiful,' she says.

Penelope raises her eyes to the tall part of the mirror to behold this woman with her dark lustrous hair, her round face and the not unpretty grey eyes.

'The beach,' she says rising, causing the older woman's hand to plop limply down.

'Must we?' Gwen asks.

Chapter Nineteen

'Hi, sis.'

'Dermot?'

'Yeah.'

'Where are you?'

'Paddy's bar.'

'Paddy's bar! You mean...?'

'Yeah, I'm over here.'

There is a pause.

'Look,' he says, 'if you don't want to see me.'

'Of course I do. But you travelled all that way, just to see me?'

'Sure,' he says. 'Is a brother not entitled to visit his sister?'

'What? Of course, Dermot, but...'

'But what?'

'There's nothing wrong, is there?'

'What could be wrong?'

'But I thought...'

'I'm keeping clean if that's what you mean...'

'Clean?'

'Yeah. All that stuff, it's all in the past. I told my mates.'

'What mates?'

'My mates. I just told them when they were coked up. I just told them. I said to them, You're full of crap.'

'You never said such a thing.'

'I did. I swear, sis. You wouldn't believe the crap that comes out of some of those coke-heads.'

'You swear?'

'Sure I swear. I'm through with all that.'

'And you went to the group meetings?'

'Yeah.'

'You swear to me?'

'I told you.'

'Oh Dermot. Stay right where you are. I'll be over to you in a jiff.'

'That's okay then. I'll just be waiting here.'

And his voice, no matter what... she is so delighted, she can hardly contain herself. To hear from him, to hear him for once so... upbeat.

She buys fresh croissants on the way in the panadería, just the last two remaining after the morning purchase blitz. A strawberry tart she also purchases as it fetches her attention in the window of the adjoining pastelería. She remembers Dermot liking strawberries, the only fruit he ever ate. Thus laden, she arrives at Paddy's bar which is a smallish building situated on a slope overlooking shops and side streets and beyond to the sea. A huge shamrock dangles from a chain near the front door in what she considers an in-your-face twee type of nationalism. She imagines the clientele: soccer fans and loud drinkers cocooning themselves into a narrow patriotic bubble, not unlike the English expats in their milieu.

Inside the pub it's dark and uninviting in contrast to the bright sunny day outside. The premises are almost empty. A short stocky guy in a white apron is going around sweeping the floor and upending chairs. Dermot is standing: his back is pressed in against the ledge of the bar, with the old familiar black canvas travel bag at his feet that he's had for years, bought, she remembers, for a fiver in Clerys. On seeing her he nods, puts down his half empty glass of beer on the counter.

They hug, almost a formal hug, as if they are afraid to touch one another. Afraid of an emotional bomb exploding on contact.

'Hi, sis.'

'Let me look at you,' she says, feelings rising in her.

His eyes are of a lighter shade than Penelope's, near hazel, but they have a milky look, showing more of the whites. She had almost forgotten how tall he was, being accustomed as he was to slouch, at least six foot one when he stood up straight, but despite his height he looks malnourished. He was never a good eater; pale and pustular, she remembers him picking at his food and never eating vegetables. She takes in the thin, almost anaemic, arms protruding through his black Guinness T-shirt and a surge of protectiveness sweeps over her towards him, no matter what she had felt initially about wanting to break away. Far away from home he is, her little brother, her baby brother with that fringe of brown hair with its reddish tint which he constantly pushes back from his forehead, like it's giving him something to do. She glances down at his loafers: no socks. Casual, careless, all imply vulnerability. And he had taken the initiative, had gone to the trouble of contacting her. And her heart surges at the thought, the potential of what he could be.

'You're sure you can manage it?' she says as he slings the canvas bag over his shoulder.

'No problem.' He tries to smile but it is not Dermot to smile. It is a simulated contortion.

'We're only a few blocks away,' she says. 'When did you arrive?'

'I told you.' The incipient tone of that familiar impatience.

'Sorry. You went to see Dad?'

'Yeah.'

'You didn't.'

'Believe what you want.'

'How is he then?'

'Same as always.'

'Meaning?'

'Same as always.'

96

She knows not to pursue the matter, for the moment anyway, sensing already an edge in his voice. Bubbles of sweat appear on his forehead and the T-shirt, hanging loosely, emphasises his sunken chest; and in contrast, those heavy tight denim jeans seem to be glued onto him.

'Have you no shorts?'

'Sure,' he says, 'boxers.'

'Oh, Dermot.'

He looks in all directions shiftily as they make their way through the apartment complex, awkwardly navigating around the half-naked bodies by the pool. How out-of-place he seems. He belongs to the night, she is convinced, or to a land of cold climates and overcoats.

He tries that smile again silently showing his bad teeth and high gums, as they wait for the lift. Does he not go to the dentist? Does he not get regular check ups? Of course not; would anyone who was hooked on something think of going to a dentist? They don't speak on the lift either as they are squashed by a squad of young returning swimmers and snorkellers dripping chlorinated water onto their toes.

'Inside at last,' she says, pushing in her front door which is inclined to be stiff. 'I'll put on the fan' (which she had eventually purchased on her last visit to the centre). 'Phew, the heat really hits you, doesn't it. Do you want to take a shower?'

'Maybe later,' he says.

'Aren't you going to put your bag down?'

Slowly – reluctantly, it seems to her – he places his zipped-tight bag down on the tiled floor. He casts a cursory glance around with both hands in his pockets. God, why can't they hug properly, embrace warmly, brother and sister? He always did that: hang around with his hands in his pockets. She is prompted to say, Take your hands out of your pockets. There was never a mother to say it; always too far gone she was in her own tangent to correct him when he was small; and it was not Penelope's place to say it. Still, she realises it's such a small thing compared to the other weightier (Ramón's word) things. And her thought returns to the lane – the images will never leave her – and the state of him sprawled on the wet ground, so... pathetically. But here he is now, upright and coherent; she is glad of that, no matter what. And here she is, his older sis, and all she can do is censure him for having his hands in his pockets. But really, his hands in his pockets, his back turned to her, God, what manners, staring out the balcony down at the pool.

'Cute chicks,' he says.

'I've fresh croissants,' she says ignoring the comment; she must ignore such laddish things, she knows that, if he is to be encouraged in his sober ways (she was almost going to say righteous). 'And we can have tea. You'd like tea?'

'Whatever.' His shoulders hunch up. 'Who knows you're here?' he says.

'What? Just you and Dad I suppose, if he is aware that is; for all the difference it would make to him anyway. Why? Oh, and Sheila.'

'Sheila?'

'My agent.'

'But she doesn't come over, no?'

'No.'

They sit at the table. All the time he is avoiding eye contact with her, casting towards the balcony as if it can provide an escape route if the urge seizes him, which it could, she knows from old. There is an ethereal quality about Dermot that at any moment he could just evanesce.

'Oh, I almost forgot. I got strawberry tart,' she says. 'They have wonderful strawberries over here. Remember you always liked...'

'Great,' he says, puncturing her sentence.

But he hardly touches the tart which she sets out in neat triangular cut pieces for him. And, as for the croissant, he just picks at the flaked bits.

He takes a cigarette out of a squashed packet from his jeans and lights it with a match which he holds suspended as if not knowing what to do with it.

'I'll get a saucer,' she says.

'This will do here,' he says and he impales the tart slice with the spent match.

'Are you still working?' she says trying to hide her revulsion.

'Working?'

'In the off-licence? Are you still there?'

'No. There were vipers in that place.'

'Vipers?'

'Yeah. Had to get them out of my hair you know.'

'So, how do you... get by?'

'I'm looking around, I'll get something. Just give me a bit of time, right.'

It's not for me to give you a bit of time, she was going to say, but held it back. Instead she says, 'And Daddy, is he really...?'

'You asked me already.'

'I know.'

'He's worse, if you must know.'

'Worse? What do you mean?'

'What do I mean? He hardly recognised me the last time. He should be put away.'

'Put away! That's not a nice thing to say, Dermot.'

'Well, that's life, isn't it? It's not meant to be nice, is it? It's not candycoated like your fiction.'

'Is that what you think of my fiction?'

99

'Whatever,' he says.

'But do you think he's coping?' she says sticking to the father.

'How the fuck would I know whether he's coping or not?'

'He confided in you, Dermot.'

'Confided my ass. He just wanted an errand boy.'

'I did try to persuade him to consider the nursing home, before I left.'

'Sure you did,' he says indifferently. He's talking again with his back to her, looking out over the balcony at the cute chicks.

'I had a nice place picked out in Booterstown.'

'Ah fuck him,' Dermot says, and he flicks the butt of his cigarette over the balcony. She was about to protest about the cigarette, that it could burn someone down below, but something stops her, fear perhaps of what he would reply or do.

'We're not here to talk about him, are we?' he says.

'No, I suppose not,' she says realising that Dermot is right in his cruel sort of way.

'You can have the other bedroom while you're "looking around,"' she says sarcastically. 'That's presuming you are staying for a while.'

'We'll see.'

'And here,' she says, unravelling a spare key from a ring on the worktop.

He turns. 'You're planning on being out a lot?'

She regards him for a moment. He can't hold her gaze. He turns away. 'It's not like before, Dermot,' she says. 'We're free agents now.'

'Ha.' The sneer.

He switches on the TV and lounges in the armchair, his long legs stretched out in that lazy way of his, jeans ridden up, revealing a hairless white calf. A soccer match is on. Some South American teams. A centre forward has just scored a goal, a nice lob over the goalkeeper's head. He runs around the pitch like a headless chicken expecting plaudits no doubt, demanding and getting real live kisses from fellow males. Disgusting. Then, to her amazement, the goalscorer kneels down and runs his nose along the white line of the penalty area. 'Yeah,' shouts Dermot.

He shouts at that, and he didn't shout at the goal!

His mobile phone rings in a side pocket of his jeans – a low conspiratorial susurration. Making no excuse for the interruption, he lifts the phone to his ear and moves away onto the balcony. She watches; she would love to be able to read his lips; all writers should be lip readers; what they would gain for their plots and their dialogue; but he has, as if realising, turned from a side position to show his back to her once more.

He puts away the phone and comes into the living room, his mop of hair lifted by the fan.

'I've to meet someone,' he says.

'Meet someone? Who? I mean you've just arrived.'

'I've been here a while.'

'What? But where were you staying?'

'Here and there.'

'Dermot. Who is it you know?'

'Who knows anyone?'

'At least have a shower first,' she says. 'Is it that urgent they can't wait a while?'

The doorbell rings. He fetches up his travel bag immediately and holds it in both hands to his chest. He looks alarmed, and then accusingly to Penelope he says, 'Who is that?'

'Probably my neighbour.'

As Penelope opens the door Dermot takes himself hurriedly into the spare bedroom.

'Gwen.'

'High de high.'

'It's not a good time, Gwen.'

Gwen pokes her head in the door. 'What? You've got company?'

'Yes. My brother, he's just arrived. I'm in the middle of helping him unpack.'

'Oh well then,' she says. 'I'll call back another time.'

'You don't mind?'

'What... little old me? Why should I mind?'

'See you later then,' Penelope says, closing the door.

'You didn't have to fucking tell her it was your brother who was here,' Dermot says furiously, coming out of the bedroom, still nursing his bag in his arms.

'What difference does it make?'

'Don't give those ones any information.'

'Those ones! You don't even know her.'

He scowls. 'I saw her.'

'What are you saying, Dermot? You sound paranoiac.'

'I saw her before.'

'You saw Gwen, where?'

'I just saw her,' he shouts. 'Nosing. You understand, nosing?'

She can't sleep. Dermot has left her to ponder on a multitude of things. The practical present: where has he gone? Who has he gone to see? Who was it he spoke to on his mobile phone that required such urgent attention? When will he be back? Where was he for his 'while' before he contacted her?

She presses the light on her bedside clock: 2:35. Will he come back at all? Of course he'll come back. Isn't his precious bag locked in the wardrobe? Was it really to prevent outside thieves that he locked it away, or was it to prevent her from prying into its contents?

He is hiding something, of that she is certain, and he is hiding from somebody too, judging by the shifty way he behaved when Gwen called. He's just using his sister. Still, he brought her a Toblerone. Saying nothing, typical of him, he just left it there on his bedside table as he went out. Thoughtful. She had felt it soft from the heat and had put it in the fridge. No matter what, it was nice of him to remember that she always liked Toblerone (at weekends she'd often bring a bar home for the late movie on TV if Mother or Father weren't too intrusive; it was her comfort zone which in the early days she sometimes shared with Dermot, depending on his mood, for he was always moody). Yes, she liked her Toblerone just as he liked his strawberries, or used to, and she thinks of the slice of strawberry tart which he had left on his plate.

She rises and places his slice of tart (having cut out the piece with the spent match) beside the Toblerone in the fridge, fitting together like a brother and a sister ought. She was inclined – she'd be the first to admit, and how could she be any other way? – to look at the dark side of things, and she thinks for while of Thomas Hardy, a kindred spirit, whose novels were on her Arts

103

course in college. And Hardy was her staple diet until she discovered the escape route through the happy endings of romantic fiction. And she avoided sad endings from that moment, on reaching the conclusion (or rather on being induced to reach it) that sad people should not read sad fiction, and to subscribe to – what Sheila claims everyone wants – a happy ending.

But why then, she wonders returning to bed, were Greek tragedies popular, or Shakespearean drama for that matter, or disaster movies or love stories with lovers dying? Sheila had no time for stories like that. She deemed them aberrations. So anyone who followed those sad stories must be abnormal in some way.

Still – and her thoughts veer back to Dermot – he did look better since the last time she saw him. And he did say he was 'clean'. She sighs. Oh dear, this sleep business. She tries to count backwards in Spanish from a hundred: ciento, noventa y nueve, noventa y ocho, noventa y siete – it worked the last time she was animated – noventa y siete. No, she already said that. Oh, it's no good.

She throws the sheet off her. The fan is whirring as in the half light she goes to the fridge once more and takes out the Toblerone. Why is chocolate such a comfort? she wonders. Why is it portrayed as preferable to sex on those TV and film ads? It satisfies something inside one, some irrational craving (which is always female of course, according to her father). It should be hard by now, the chocolate, but, to her surprise, she finds it still soft as she presses into it. It's been what? At least three hours since she put it into the fridge. It doesn't make sense.

She opens a side pyramid. A sachet of white powder falls onto the floor. She examines the inside of the box. More sachets. All sachets in fact, she realises, as she tumbles them out onto the table, switching on her table lamp.

So, she exclaims, he lied. I should've known better than to believe that he was 'clean'. One is to presume Dermot had left it on the bed by accident in his hurry out. He had meant to bring it with him for his own use or someone else's, to peddle, to deal, that's what he's at – let's not make any bones about the matter. And she wonders what it meant to sell a line of coke or 'do a line with Charlie', what she'd heard at that party. And she wondered, how so many words are like that, with their semantic shifts? And she reflects on the language of her first novel. It seems so innocent now, so mono, so one-dimensional, as if life were like that, smelling of roses.

She squeezes the sachets back into the carton, seals the pyramid and returns the Toblerone to his bedside table between his Hugo Boss aftershave and a red tin of talcum powder.

Cocaine. How innocent it sounds like a variation of cocoa, that wholesome night-time beverage; she can still picture it in the kitchen at home, growing up on cocoa and the picture on the cover of the box of the sister and brother, arms outstretched, like a stairs showing how they grow.

She goes out to her table, plugs in her laptop, connects to the Internet and searches. Even Coca Cola, she reads, contained cocaine until it was taken out of that drink in 1905. South America, Africa, Gibraltar, the areas through which it travels to find its way to the Costas. When it is smoked, it reaches the brain in four seconds. The image of Dermot in the gutter keeps flashing before her, yes, like it's integrated into the web search itself. 'Clean, my eye,' she exclaims. 'I bet he never went to even one of those group sessions.'

She presses 'Continue': My night out accessory so neat in its little white envelope like a handkerchief in a pocket, she added, embellishing the piece like part of your attire. Coke makes your eyes sparkle, and she sees Topless Jane. Yes, her eyes did sparkle, for a dimwit, she adds cruelly, and the thought: are they all users? All those – again cruelly – beach bums, what Gwen terms the hammock dawdlers?

But surely not all, not Ramón. God, she is going to see him again. At this very moment she would like to talk to him, to feel his cool presence beside her. She could confide in him; she is sure of it. She is to see him tomorrow. Yes, they had agreed. He is to show her the old quarter. How many people realise there is an old quarter to Felicidad? Where the locals live in little white cottages, where he lives; and he will show her the primary school where he teaches.

Yes, she says resolutely, looking towards the bright moon shining in her balcony: she has her own life to lead. Was it not the reason why she came to Spain after all, to escape the emotional stranglehold of a father? And she wasn't now going to be entangled by his son. No, thank you.

She was making progress over here after all, at least with her new-found freedom. She has her own apartment (Sheila's advice was sound in that respect). She can come and go as she pleases. And with Ramón there is hope. A looking forward instead of a life lived dwelling on past recriminations.

And it could be added, a sort of equilibrium was being almost reached in her life (she can see her fingertips reaching high towards the ceiling, trying to touch its stippled surface) but then, damn him, unbalanced once more – how quickly, how easily – by the arrival of her brother. No, he will not distort the balance. Not any more. She will not allow it.

It will take time, she knows, to shake all that stuff out of her head, but she is determined not to regress into that negative low esteem world. She is resolute; she will not let them do that to her. No way.

Besides, she is not her brother's keeper, no more than she is her father's keeper, although a little self-doubt creeps into her self-conscious soul with her remembering of the biblical injunction – she did honour him in so far as she was able. But not any more. Every hand carries its imperfection. She has done her duty.

And Dermot, he is no longer a child; he is responsible for his own life. Still – curse these thoughts – she can't help herself feeling for him especially in a foreign country. He is exposed despite his bravura and – yes indeed – the downright bad manners. He's running scared of something. What is it she feels herself being sucked into? How did he get embroiled into a seedy underworld over here? The web search shows the greater demand follows the tide. That's what Dermot is doing.

She rises from her tubular chair and goes to the sideboard and pours a generous measure from the remaining airport brandy into her only tumbler. Oh God, she starts; is she becoming like her mother with her fondness for the brandy? And she pours half the measure back again into the bottle. She will have to buy more glasses: if she had guests, what would they drink from? And she is thinking in particular of Gwen and Ramón.

Hennessy – those Irish names spread across Europe. The brandy hits her gut like a flame. She locates a bottle of Sprite in the fridge to dilute it. The word dilute, she thinks for a moment. Have I diminished it by diluting it, by making it more palatable? A diluted brandy costs more than a straight brandy. Strange that. Drugs she always feared, the irrationality it brought out in people.

When she was coming down Crow's Lane that night on leaving Dermot, a man approached her, she remembers, a young dishevelled fellow with a menacing look. She was convinced he would do her an injury; and for a terrifying moment she thought that she would never get out of that lane; and she knew her brother was back there wallowing in his own spittle, and she knows – and she feels her anger rising – that he would have continued to sit there impotently, and she would have been at the mercy of that apparent predator. It turned out the fellow just walked past her. But that realisation afterwards, she remembers, was nearly as depressing as finding Dermot the way he was.

A noise from next door disquiets her. Those paper-thin walls, she never judged. It is the opposite side to Gwen's. A muffled scream. Was it playful or terror-stricken? She could not decipher. The word Fuck, male-uttered. And argumentative voices, heavily accented. The prostitutes, according to Gwen who spoke of glimpsing their pale morning visages, are like vampires shunning daylight. And yet were they all pale? Were they not some of those bronzed ones on the beach? Friends of Charlie?

And she looks at her drink as she swirls it in her glass. The mixture. And she thinks of the sachets of powder. Are they mixed? Is that what Dermot does, mix powders like an apothecary? which of course is a career he could have taken up. Oh, if you could see me now, Daddy. But how did he learn about the Costas? From Crow's Lane to the Costa del Sol. What was the attraction? Increasing demand yes, of course, with the burgeoning of the non-indigenous population in the heathen life of the Costas.

Sitting with her drink back at her desk, she presses the mouse to banish the screen saver of the multicoloured Rubik's cube. She reads: It is sometimes cut with glucose and talcum powder to increase its weight and get a higher price, and other ingredients are sometimes added such as petrol, caustic soda and battery acid.

Chapter Twenty One

She is early. The sleepless night had forced her up. All that waiting for the prodigal brother who never returned. She wants to banish him now from her mind with a breath, blow him away like the extinguishing of a candle, and she breathes in deeply filling out her white T-shirt with fresh morning air. She had followed the road towards the church, as Ramón had told her, which took her to the square and the little fountain in view of the white casitas.

She sits on the low granite wall surrounding the fountain. Plain white spray, so cool and refreshing to feel some of it on her face, the white jets shooting up in a cascade like an upsidedown waterfall, like something in abandon, what she longs for, what she would wish for, and in abundance, like water should be abundant in the world.

There are a few stone benches occupied around the courtyard, one with an old woman resting from her shopping, checking inside her supermarket plastic bag. Has she forgotten something? Have we all forgotten something, like Dermot forgetting to return? A worker in navy blue overalls cycles past, a plank of wood balanced on his handlebars.

She hears the sound; yes, it is of dominoes coming from the little bar across the way: weathered old men perched vigilantly upright, she can just make out. She finds it exhilarating to hear the crash of the dominoes descending onto tables like a thunder roar wakening the senses. A couple of the old men with caps flung back far on their heads in hoarse voices are exclaiming excitedly like children. Oh, the wonder never ceases.

She looks at the sky. She thinks up her colours. Blue: delphinium, hydrangea, ceanothus. Yes, ceanothus blue, that will do for today. And she presses her lips on her freshly applied, cherry crystal lipstick. Oh, all these musings, making oneself up as one goes along. Yes. She looks around at the quiet, quotidian life of the old quarter. She hears the sound of a bell. Yes, the little church on the hill, small, neat in its adobe brick, blending with the countryside, not at all oppressive like those big city cathedrals.

He appears out of a blink of light in a short-sleeved yellow shirt and white jeans. He smiles, takes her hand, helping her up from the wall. 'You were waiting long?'

'No, not very. I wanted to come early to look around. To get a sense of... you.'

'A sense of me? Ah.' He smiles again and they both look in the direction of the little cottages entwining with their whitewashed walls adjoined with intricate black wrought iron gates (bearing designs as delicate as lace), and earthen pots of red geraniums, standing sentry at the front doors.

'The street,' she says, 'is very narrow.'

'That's a good thing, don't you think,' he says, 'to keep out the traffic. The building over there,' he points.

She looks at the small flatroofed building surrounded by silver railings and a little concrete yard to its side.

'It's the primary school where I teach.'

'That's the place?'

'Yes. Closed now for the summer.'

'I should've guessed you were a teacher.'

'Why? Why should you have guessed that?'

She shrugs. 'I don't know, just something about you. A caring disposition.'

'You flatter me.'

'Are there many in your class?'

'Oh yes. Not all Spaniards either. I have many of the expatriado children. English, Irish.'

'Yes.'

'Yes. And now,' he says taking her hand, 'I will show you where my mother sleeps.'

He leads her up a steep hill at the back of the white cottages. She sees the cemetery, all the white marble glittering in the late morning sunshine. Are they really dead, those people? she wonders. It seems a travesty on such a bright sunny day.

'You have suncream?' he says.

'Yes.'

'You should put it on.' The sun is at its hottest now, vertically over their heads. 'Your fair skin,' he says, stroking her arm.

Penelope takes suncream from her canvas bag. She always carries it when going about with her bottle of water (and her aforementioned felt-tip pens). She applies the suncream to her face and arms self-consciously as he gazes. Is he looking for a spot she has missed? 'My legs are fine,' she says.

'No,' he says.

'What?'

'You must cover them too.'

'Oh, all right. Just to please you.'

'No,' he says.

'What?'

'Not to please me. Let me.'

'You?' A half laugh; isn't he being a bit fresh now?

'Sit down on the rock.' The command, the voice; in another language it would be considered stentorian, but not with his caring manner. A flat slab of granite, shaped like a chair, she sits on. One leg (what is propelling her?) from her pink cotton shorts with toes pointing outward she offers to him. He squirts the lotion – God, don't let it make a farty sound – which flows freely into his broad concave palm. Starting at her foot, oh so softly, the

111

palm sets out on its maiden voyage upwards. Oh, was the milk ever softer on Cleopatra's limbs?

'And the other.'

They pass through the tall silver gate of the cemetery, and he veers her to the left along a narrow path by a wall with urns placed in niches. There are a few people scattered about: an old man praying over a grave with his beret crinkled in his hand, and a couple of women in headscarves arched with little rakes and hand trowels tidying the plots.

'Buenos días, Ramón,' the women say in unison as he and Penelope make their way through corridors of graves until he stops opposite a plain white marble tombstone with gold lettering and a photograph of a woman.

'This is your mother?'

'Yes.'

Penelope stoops down to behold the image of an attractive dark-haired woman with smiling black eyes. And yes, she muses, there is a resemblance – but only slight – to herself, in the wave of the hair and the shape of the face. 'She is so young-looking,' she says, standing up.

'Yes,' he says.

'How did she die?'

'She was stabbed to death.'

'What?'

'Through her heart, by a drug addict.'

'Oh my God?'

'A crazed man on the seafront went to rob her, demanded her purse. When she resisted, he stabbed her.'

'Oh Ramón, I'm so sorry.'

He is silent. She looks sideways at him. He is praying, his lips supplicating. What are they saying? He is communing with his mother, gaining sustenance from her. This is where his source is, she realises now, his fountain. He blesses himself.

'The dead don't die,' he says. 'They look on and help.'

'Do you visit here often?'

'Oh yes. And now,' he says as if the matter is over, 'I will show you my house,' and he adds, 'that is if you would like.'

She presses his arm. 'Yes. I would like that very much.'

'Do you have sisters and brothers?' she asks as they walk down the slope, holding hands, towards the white cottages.

'No,' he says, 'there was no chance.'

'Chance?'

'Opportunity. My father went away, left us at an early stage.'

'Oh, I'm sorry.'

'No, no, it was okay because I then did not have to share my mother with anyone. So you see,' he says triumphantly, 'there is always good that comes out of bad.'

'You really believe that?'

'What? That good comes out of bad? Yes. I do believe that.'

'But your mother, Ramón. I'm still aghast at what happened to her.'

'She is fresh in my memory always; it was only three years ago; not like the past of those ancestors you talk about. I can still see her going about her daily chores, her hands moving. I can see her walking [he is wistful, looking into the distance], walking on her way, as we are walking now, charlando, chatting yes, to a neighbour. She is smiling on her way to the market, carrying her old fishing basket. She is waving now, waving to me. I am a little boy standing at my bedroom window, wiping my breath from the... window pane – yes, that is the word isn't it? – looking out. The wave of someone,' he says, 'coming from...'

She gives a little cough. Is he disturbed? she wonders.

113

'You think I'm extraño?'

'No. Of course not.'

'Yes, you do.'

'Well, perhaps a little.'

'We all are a little strange, aren't we, in our depths?'

'Yes,' she says. 'I suppose we are. In our depths.' And she feels for the space where her pearls should be.

He holds the gate open for her which spring-shuts, she would like to think, to keep in all the ghosts. They meander down the slope back towards the village, with her arm linking his, unhurried, looking at the ground, pushing a stone aside with her white sandal. Two souls pondering, communing silently perhaps. She feels the pulse in his arm. She is connected. But does Ramón accept that his mother is a ghost or does he think she is something other?

'How come you became a life guard?' she says, trying to steer thoughts away from the cemetery.

'Because I like the sea. It has a hidden power beyond our imagining.'

'Like you,' she says

'Me?' He laughs. 'I don't think so.'

The little white cottage is situated in a narrow cobblestoned street in the middle of a terrace without frontage, and with bougainvillaea climbing to the orange tiles of its saddle-back roof.

The first thing she notices on going inside is the low ceiling. She looks at Ramón. Does he realise he's stooped? Is he so conditioned? Such a small house to produce such a big man.

'You see it over there in the corner, her basket?' he says, pointing into a tiny but amply stocked pine kitchen.

'Yes,' she says, beholding a broken wicker basket. 'What is it like here?' she says, 'in winter?'

'In winter,' he says, 'it is the best time. You can see the sand on the beach. You can hear the ocean roar like el toro.'

There's an oak bookcase crammed with books and papers in the circular sitting room and a green Colección Austral paperback lying on the coffee table: *El Sentimiento Trágico de la Vida* by Miguel de Unamuno. She lifts it up, careens through its pages.

'Take it with you,' he says. 'Read it. Unamuno is a great thinker.'

'If I am able to understand it.'

'You will. The Spanish is very clear.'

'Thank you. I'll give it a try,' she says, slipping the book into her canvas bag. But the tragic sentiment of life, she thinks, musing on the title, does she really want to read about that?

'Now,' he says, 'for lunch, we will go to the top of the hill.'

'But,' she says, 'we were up there already, were we not?'

'No no,' he says, 'we did not go to the top, that was only the beginning where the cemetery is. Farther up we will go another way, by the goat path. ¿De acuerdo?'

She smiles. 'De acuerdo.'

He helps to pull her along the stony rise flanked by fields of sunflowers and olive groves, and farther up the more arid parts and rocky terrain to the world of the goats, some of whom are perched observing them like sentries on the rocks, while others root around the undergrowth, heads down, bells ringing from their necks.

A couple of goats trail them, getting closer to Penelope, making her cling to Ramón.

'You are afraid of the goats?' he says.

'Of their horns, yes.'

'Come,' he says, and he whooshes her up onto a high flat rock. 'You are safe now.'

'But the goats are good climbers,' she says, unconvinced.

'I will... what is the word? I will shoo them away if they come near. And now,' by way of distracting her, he says pointing, 'look at the view. You see all the towers of Felicidad how small, how insignificant they are in the distance.'

'Oh, and look,' she says, 'I see the sea.'

'Of course.'

'How different it looks to the night time.'

'The night time? You...?'

'Yes I walked by the beach the other night.'

'On your own?'

'Yes.'

'It is dangerous.'

'I didn't perhaps realise that at the time. I was thinking of other things.'

'What things?'

'Oh, just things,' she says. 'But anyway I saw a boat coming in on the waves with what I figured were illegal immigrants.'

'In Felicidad,' he says incredulously, 'you saw this?'

'Yes.'

'No. That is not what you saw.'

'What do you mean, Ramón?' She tugs at his sleeve.

'Illegal immigrants don't come into Felicidad. They choose ports nearer to the coast of Africa. What you saw were drug peddlers.'

'Oh,' she says. 'Are you sure?'

'Yes. The good and the bad, the sea takes them all.'

'I didn't realise.'

'It's happening a lot. It is very bad for our country. The big

116

ships, they come from Colombia with huge quantities of cocaine, and in Africa they load them onto smaller boats and get into Spain that way. What you saw.'

'Should I have reported it? Should I have gone to the police?' No sooner has she said this than she thinks of Dermot and his connection, no matter how small, with this sordid enterprise.

'Yes,' he says, 'but you were not to know.'

Think of a father: of one who disempowers you, who disables you, who takes away your facility for action; who saps you of a desire to go forward; of one who would have you hide away in a cupboard; who would have you give up the ghost. But now that she feels away from the source (that poisoned fountain) of her pain, she can explain her self. She can enter every room of herself without fear, and explore her own mansion without anyone slamming the doors shut. She can test the furniture, recline here, sit up there, stand bold wherever she wishes. This little bit of Penelope Eames that is in the small anteroom, what has she found there? All the parts of herself to be marvelled at. Piece them together. Make herself whole.

But why had she not spoken to Ramón as she had intended, to confide in him about Dermot, and her father and indeed her whole sorry family? The opportunity was there especially when he spoke of the drug peddlers. Why didn't she take the cue and mention the raw realities? Was she afraid of losing him before she had even gained him? (for she was indeed growing fond of him). Was she fearful of foregoing a chance for love? That he would find her with too much baggage? Too much weightedness? Is it possible? And she thinks of the high rock they had stood on ('on top of the world,' Ramón had said) – how strange to be carrying the world on one's shoulders while simultaneously standing on it. But no, she did not confide in Ramón because she is a romantic at heart, she concludes (or more plausibly, wishes to be), not just a romantic novelist. She does not want him to think she is carrying the world on her shoulders, but rather the moon and the stars. She knows he sees her in that light. How does she know? By the way he looks at her, by the gentleness he shows towards her; oh, and by the way he whooshed her up on the rock (his hands resting so warmly on her hips). To so disclose, she would be afraid of disappointing him. No, she would not do that. She will confine the raw realities for the moment at least to the depths of solitary sleepless nights. She could bear it; it's a price she is willing to pay for the happy calm she experiences with Ramón.

But plasters are needed. 'I always carry plasters,' she said to Gwen when Gwen cut her finger while slicing the portion of strawberry tart abandoned by Dermot. 'It's only a nick,' Gwen said, showing less concern about her finger than she had previously shown about her nail. 'Still, there's enough red in the strawberry,' Penelope said, but only half jokingly. And Gwen looked at her with a strange look, and Penelope was conscious of it. She was positively bathing in her, milking her for every shade of feeling she may have towards her, as Penelope, gentle as always, whether it was ministering to her cantankerous father's ailments (she was dutiful no matter what), or to her school-kid brother the time he too cut his finger when opening a tennis ball tin. Not that she ever thought of herself in such a light, of the nursing or caring type. She was merely doing her duty, performing a humanitarian act, what most people she believed would do in a similar situation. And it was not that she expected anything in return, for indeed she remembers (as if it were yesterday) Dermot pulling away. 'Hurry up,' he said gruffly, taking his sibling for granted, and the mother who should have been doing these things, she knew, was paralytic in the parlour.

But Gwen was temporising; she was not pulling away; she was gazing lovingly – surely not the word (but yes, it is the word) – into Penelope's eyes.

'There,' Penelope said, but still the finger lingered. 'Gwen.'
'Sorry.'
And she remembers her sighing as she rose from the tubular

119

chair. And when Gwen swanned away rather enigmatically, her actions, it seemed to Penelope, were now becoming as ambivalent as her vocabulary.

She walks out to her balcony, breathing in the cooler evening air, the sun having moved, and she thinks of her mother. What had made her an alcoholic? Such a hopeless case ever since Penelope was a teenager, and earlier if the truth were known, if things hadn't been hidden (empty naggin bottles in cupboards under soft underwear). Was it because she believed in what her husband told her, that she was useless, weak, feeble, sentimental, all those words he had for her and bandied them about without shame, even in public. She could not compete. She was not an educated woman. (Was that why he had married her perhaps, so that he could exploit her apparent inferiority?) How could she compete with such an eminent personage? And when you can't compete, what do you do? You succumb. God, she hated her. She hated her mother for succumbing.

And now here she is in her own mind, an ageing virgin, who wants to break away from such a bind, who craves to make love before dying like some of those annual flowers shedding their seed at their point of expiry; and she is thinking (womanly as her father would say) like the heroine of her first novel with its sentimental romanticism ingrained in her. And that she had to break away from the tight little nuclear families of Dundrum where she did not fit in (where does a single woman fit in?). These microcosms so fulfilled, self-satisfied until a little chink, of course, appears. And, smiling wryly, she thinks of the plaster and how ill-prepared are people for the eventualities of life, and how easy it is to be left bereft in the outer world, the macrocosm, where one must trawl around looking for a plaster.

Yes, that image, it works; she writes it into her notebook to use imaginatively perhaps at a later date. And what was that other phrase her father used? An article of faith – was it he who coined the term to force acceptance of his hypotheses on his minions? Words and their polysemy. Professor Eames jocularly (a rare moment) referred to his undergraduate female students presenting to him their articles of faith, their supposed theses of insights (his insights!) into morbid anatomy, and it was her introduction – she knows it now – to the world of nuances and double speak, the nudge nudge extra-nuptial metaphors of males. The first time she heard it was when it was delivered with venomous glee over the dinner table that winter night long ago (when Ramón saw the sand on the beach and listened to the ocean roar), when she was scarce out of her teens, and she puzzled over its meaning, thinking in her innocence it may even have possessed the possibility of religious connotations until, with her continually going on about it, in a moment of sober exasperation, her mother set her right.

Her mother knew all along.

Chapter Twenty Three

The candles have burnt low on Gwen's cherry wood table; minute remains of salmon adorn her Queen jubilee plates. Penelope had agreed or rather surrendered to her neighbour's persistent prodding to spend a night in. Gwen is clearly embellished with her glossy plum fingernails, matching lips and galaxy purple eye-shadow, but conflicting with her garnet sky silk. Gwen gazes, her eyes glazed over from the wine, the sheen reflecting off the silverware. Uncomfortable, Penelope extricates herself by looking around the flat: it is a facsimile of her own, the same size living room and kitchen and balcony, except Gwen's is more east facing and gets more of the early sun, and the walls are all white unlike Penelope's cerulean blue – the little one can see of them, for they are almost erased with cheap copies of cheaper paintings (did she buy them all in the one store?) of horses and dogs and unrecognisable landscapes of nowhereland. Oh, and there's one over the fridge which is not too bad, granted it is only a photograph, of high coniferous trees in a mountain setting.

'That photo,' Gwen says, noticing Penelope looking, 'my sister sent me from Canada. I was going to go over to them after my divorce.'

'Them?' Penelope says.

'She's married and has two kids in a place called London, would you believe? She invited me. I was all set. I dreamed of a place in fact where the pine trees would be taller than the pylons in Spitalfields. I did actually go for a visit. It was winter; maybe that's what did it; the cold and the snow turned me off. The thing is I got chilblains.'

'Drink your wine,' Penelope says as she sips hers.

'Did you ever get chilblains?'

'No.'

'So,' she continues, 'all things considered, I opted for Spain. We need warmth in our lives, don't we?' She caresses Penelope's arm across the table. 'Don't we, Pen?'

'Yes. I suppose we do.'

Gwen smiles. 'Suppose. You're always supposing.'

'Look, Gwen,' she says drawing her hand away, 'I don't know if you are...'

'Bi and bi, is what you mean?' Gwen lilts.

'Sorry, I shouldn't...'

She pats Penelope's hand. She sighs. 'I don't know what I am,' she says. 'Just a person seeking companionship. Is that too awful?'

'Of course not,' Penelope says. 'Look, I've nothing against gay or even bi people.'

'Ah, that word *even*,' Gwen says.

'What I mean...'

'It's okay,' Gwen says.

'It's just I'm heterosexual.'

'How do you know?'

'What do you mean how do I know?'

'I mean how can one ever be sure what one is. I thought I was heterosexual too until I got married. Nobody is anything; that's my conclusion. All those words, hetero, bi, doughnut-bumpers.'

'Doughnut-bumpers?' Penelope laughs.

'They're just labels. Limitations. Don't be anything,' she says, or rather commands. 'Just be you. You are beautiful, you know.'

'You already told me that.'

'Sorry, but it's worth repeating.'

'Please, Gwen.'

'Do I embarrass you?'

'Frankly, yes.'

Gwen moves away, drawing her arms into herself. 'The thing

123

is, it was soon after the divorce, soon after I came over here to Spain, that I met someone.' She sighs. 'But it was only a holiday fling for her. She returned to England. We wrote to each other for a while. Oh, how I used to live for the arrival of her letters, the scent of her pages. It was such a beautiful scent. What was it? But her husband...'

'Found out?'

''Er 'usband,' she says in exaggerated Cockney, 'was a gentleman; 'e always removed 'is 'at before 'itting a lady.'

'I see,' says Penelope.

'Men,' says Gwen.

'Not all men.'

'Don't be taken in, Penelope.'

'You mean Ramón.'

'The devil you know.'

'Really Gwen, you're so... insular. You live in this country and you don't even try to learn a word of Spanish.'

'Not me,' Gwen says.

'And what about Charlie Eliot?'

'Ah, Charlie?'

'He's a man. Why do you defend him? What did Charlie do for you?'

'He was kind to me when I came over here first.'

'Him, kind?'

'Yes, but,' she laughs, 'they change with the seasons, the Costa people, like the birds. But...' she says seriously, reaching once more for Penelope's hand, which Penelope does not resist this time...'don't ever be too sure.'

'Too sure?'

'You know what I mean.'

'I think I'm sure.'

'Sure you're sure,' Gwen says and she rises abruptly from the table. 'Your brother,' she says with her back to Penelope as she searches for something in the sideboard, 'is he over for long?'

'Oh, no,' Penelope says fazed by the question. 'I wouldn't say he'll be here for long. He's not really a sunworshipper. He'll get fed up, I expect, pretty soon.'

She's afraid to say any more about Dermot after the last time. Gwen is scraping something. Is she listening at all?

'Will he be staying with you all the time then?'

'I don't think so. He's got friends.'

'I see,' Gwen says, turning around.

'What on earth are you doing?' Penelope says.

Gwen places a saucer of white powder and two plastic straws on the table.

'Would you like to do a line with me, Pen?'

'Definitely not.'

Gwen's eyes continue to implore with the ambiguity of her words. 'People are entitled to their little sweeteners.'

'That's hardly what I'd call them.'

'Do I shock you?'

'What do you think?'

'That's twice then,' she says. 'Oh dearie me.' She lilts, 'Torture my nipples with short sharp thistles. You shouldn't be shocked. Everyone on the Costa's using it. It's only a few lines.'

She brandishes her credit card to separate the lines. 'I prefer to use this,' she says, 'to a primitive razor blade. You saw it at the party, surely? The horizontal mirrors in the Ladies?'

'I didn't use the Ladies.'

'You're not a goody-goody-two-shoes, are you, Penelope?'

She remembers Gwen, come to think of it now, using the Ladies a couple of times that night at the party. And the way she was enquiring about Dermot would suggest perhaps she knew something. And he talking about her nosing. And she thinks alarmingly, could what Gwen was snorting then and is snorting in front of her now so openly, so nonchalantly, have been supplied by her own brother?

'Don't worry,' Gwen says, 'it's only on occasions I indulge. Like now in the intimacy of...'

'What intimacy?'

'Of friendship,' she says. 'We are friends?'

'Of course, but...'

'And sometimes I indulge too for the opposite reason, when we're not the Mae West, you know, when the pain gets too hard to bear.'

Pain, Penelope wonders. What pain? And she thinks of the lump that had been in her breast. Perhaps Gwen is suffering secretly in some similar fashion or worse.

'What pain?'

Gwen sighs. 'You know, being away.'

'You miss England then?'

'Of course I miss England.'

'But you are a free person, Gwen. You can return there anytime you wish.'

'To what?' She frowns. 'There is nothing there for me. The thing is it's just nostalgia. You're sure you won't try it?' she says proffering the spare straw to Penelope.

'Do you know where that stuff comes from?' Penelope says accusingly, brushing aside the straw. 'Do you have any idea of the ramifications...?'

'Ramifications?' Gwen smiles. 'No, I don't want to know about any ramifications,' she says with a clear distaste for the word. 'If we were to go into the ramifications of everything we wouldn't even drink tea, would we, or carry our crocodile skin handbags?' She snorts again, breathing in deeply up her right nostril. 'You surprise me, Pen.'

126

'I surprise you?'

'Yes. You are so innocent. That's why Charlie...'

'Charlie? So, that's it, that's the favour he did for you. Got you onto drugs.'

'He's all right is Charlie. He just follows his John Thomas wherever it leads, like most men and, after all, no matter what they say about him he is a Bow Bells boy. We have to stick together over here you know. He saw that I didn't want for anything. He's good like that, helping people when their chips are down. When I first arrived here, boy, were my chips down, being as I was in the throes of divorce proceedings. I appreciate things like that,' Gwen says, 'the little things, little thoughtful things making me feel part of a community you know?'

'Community!' Penelope says. 'You call that a community, druggies and libertines?'

'Expats,' she says, snorting on the left nostril. She looks up. 'Oh, Pen, I really like you. You don't mind my saying?'

'I don't mind at all,' Penelope says, 'but it's not you that's saying it.'

'What?'

'You're on a high, Gwen. It's the cocaine that's talking.'

'You Irish,' she says spitting out the words. 'You can't take a compliment.'

'Look, Gwen...'

'I used to harm myself,' she says.

'Gwen, you don't have to go there.'

'A fat spotty teenager yeah, that's what I was. I had this weird notion yeah. We do have weird notions as teenagers, don't we? Had this weird notion that cutting would make the flab leak out and I'd be made thin. Mad.'

'We all have different ways of coping,' Penelope says quite at a loss as to how to respond.

'Yes,' Gwen says, 'and what was yours, or did you need one? Sorry, I'm being fucking cruel.'

'Oh, I needed one,' Penelope says.

'I still need one,' Gwen says. 'That's what he kept on about. The weight.'

'Who?'

'My ex.'

'I'm still looking,' Penelope says, thinking of the sticking plaster.

'You'll do all right,' Gwen says resignedly. 'You don't have that problem. You'll have your fling with handsome Ray.'

'You think that's all it is, a fling?'

'Only you can answer that.'

'I can't answer it, at least not yet. It's too soon.'

'But we'll continue to be friends, won't we?' She squeezes Penelope's hand.

'Of course we will,' Penelope says, feeling for her no matter what, the lost voice.

Penelope moves towards the door. Gwen draws close to her; stands for a moment silently; cheek, nose, skin almost... touching.

Chapter Twenty Four

'Where were you?' she says.

'What's the big deal? I was on a night out, all right?'

'A night out? Would you believe three nights out?'

'So what? We're free agents. You said that yourself.'

'Yeah, but we could communicate, Dermot. I was lying awake...'

He shrugs.

'... waiting for you to return. You never said, I mean you never told me when you'd be back.'

'You don't have to stay awake for me.'

'And look at you, still in that dirty T-shirt.'

'Chill out,' he says, 'I'm grabbing that shower now.'

She sits at her glass table listening to the gushing jets of the shower. She should be working; she should be able to ignore him; let him come and go as he wishes. That press interview will be coming up soon, and she will have nothing prepared. And that article she was asked to write about the expats, she emailed it off to Sheila the other day, and she wonders how it will be received. She just gave her impressions as she saw them, mentioning the prostitutes, the drugs, the parties, the smugglers coming into the bay; she was critical of the microcosm in which the expats dwelt, and exile and loneliness (and she thought of Gwen as the paradigm there), real concerns gleaned through the gloss. But there was so much more she could have said were it not for the word limitation. She could have explored that hidden world more fully, and that outer world, the great peninsula of Spain with its vibrant life and culture almost ignored. How can people live like that, was her conclusion, how can we interface with other communities and races, share in a universal humanity by living myopically in tight little enclaves like myriad Gibraltars peppered on the great map?

She's about to open her laptop when she hears him singing. She can't believe the words she's hearing; he never had a sonorous voice; it's more of a I want-to-be-heard shout:

'All your dreams are made
When you're chained to a mirror and a razor blade.'

But does he mean them, those words or is it just the song, the provocation? No, she is making excuses for him. A person doesn't sing such words without...

He opens the door of the bathroom, an apparition through the steam, hair dripping water, all skin and bone and paleness and angularity, with her white bath towel knotted around his waist.

'What are you at?' he says brushing back his moist fringe as she searches for signs: needle marks on arms, stomach, torso? Nothing but a tattoo of a naked girl named Natasha on his left biceps, lying prone, that simulates sexual action as his arm moves.

'Disgusting. Where did you get that?' she says, holding up his arm.

'Cool what?' he says.

'And who is this Natasha?'

'Ah Natasha, poor Natasha,' he says rubbing his hand over her.

'Stop playing games with me, Dermot.'

'Playing games?' He looks bemused. 'Who's playing games?'

'You left a Toblerone behind you.'

'What?'

'On your bed.'

He hurries into the bedroom leaving droplets of water on the tiles. She waits, standing by the glass table, fidgeting with the space where her necklace should be. She hears a ruffling, and Dermot reappears with the Toblerone.

'For you, sis. I left it for you.'

She opens it, tears away the foil. 'Chocolate.'

He laughs. 'Of course chocolate, what did you think it was?'

And for a crazy moment she wonders had she been mistaken. Was her fiction taking over from her reality?

His mobile phone summons him to his bedroom. She hears his voice.

'Yeah… I am sure…Where? What time? Okay.'

A moment later he is strutting out the door of the bedroom in a Day-Glo green T-shirt carrying a large black plastic bag folded over in two.

'You're going out again. You're hardly in.'

'I've got to see someone.'

'Again?'

'Yeah.'

'For what? Who have you got to see, Dermot?'

'Why all these questions? You're doing my head in.' He places both hands – the plastic bag cushioning one – on either side of his head. 'Do I ask you for what? Why you came to Spain, what you're up to?'

'We have to talk, Dermot. You can't just use me like this.'

'Use you. I'm your brother.'

'I came to Spain to get away from…'

'Me ? Isn't that it? You want me to go, to get out of your hair.'

'I didn't say that, Dermot. It's just...' and she finds herself becoming emotional, 'I have my life to lead too after all the...'

'Fine,' he says. 'You live your life.'

She is watching from her balcony as a worker in wine overalls (the Complex uniform colours) rakes debris out of the swimming pool, when her mobile phone rings its William Tell tune.

'Hi, Sheila,' she says despondently, for she thought it might have been Dermot.

'How are youuuuu?'

'I'm fine, Sheila.'

'I'll cut straight to the chase. Tiffany Pringle phoned me and I'm sorry but she can't use your article on the expats.'

'Why not?'

'She complained about its content and... intent; she even used the word intent, yes.'

'Intent?'

'Basically she's saying it's not romantic – what I keep telling you, Penelope.'

'But it's truthful.'

'Oh I know all that, but it needs a bit of glamour for Pete's sake. It's full of gloom and doom. People want a bit of glam, a bit of romance. Look at all the glossy magazines that sell like hot cakes. Why?'

'I don't know why.' She never did know why. Glossy magazines were for flicking through (no need even to disengage the stuck pages because it will always be more of the same) in seconds and thrown into the bin.

'Because of a bit of scan certainly,' Sheila is saying, 'but glam fundamentally. You didn't write about the beautiful people. Penelope, are you there?'

'Yes, I'm listening.'

'Anyway, forget about that article now. It's not the end of the world.'

'I certainly hope not.'

'And Tiffany still wants to go ahead with the interview regardless. Is that good news or what?'

'Yes, I suppose it is.'

'You suppose it is. Penelope, are you all right?'

'I'm fine.'

'Tiffany will be over on Tuesday next with the camera crew. We want to make a good impression.'

'I'll try.'

'Thata girl, and not too much serious stuff, right?'

'Right.'

'Well, adios, amigo.'

'Amiga.'

'Pardon.'

'It's amiga.'

'Well, adios anyway.'

Chapter Twenty Six

'We can move down to a quieter spot today,' Gwen says, 'but only if you like. It isn't far. I discovered it in my perambulations.'

'Really?' Penelope says.

She smiles at Gwen with her canvas bag strapped to her shoulder and her book, *Tipping the Velvet* by Sarah Waters, sticking out by design, Penelope is convinced.

She laughs. She can't help laughing, for it is her funny half hour which she occupies every so often (as it happened with Ramón). It's something that just bursts our of her for the want of crying, she knows, what with Dermot and Sheila and Tiffany Pringle hovering in the background and little Gwen here standing before her full of expectation. What is she to think? It's comical really, and she can't help laughing again, and Gwen wants to go to a ha ha ha quiet spot. Really!

'Are you all right, Penelope?'

'Am I all right? Is that what you said, in this land of the meridian heat?'

'Yeah.'

'Why wouldn't I be all right? At least everyone tells me this is the place to be all right. Of course I'm all right. I'm fine. Look at me. Let's hightail it to this quiet spot of yours.'

'You don't mind?' Gwen's eyes are bursting with joy. 'There are some naturists there.'

'You mean they're in their birthday suits?' Penelope says and she giggles again.

'You're sure you don't mind?'

'What do you take me for, Gwen, a prude?'

'I only asked. Once you don't mind. You Irish you know...'

'We Irish?'

'Well, the Pope and all that, you know?'

Penelope laughs. 'Ooh, the Pope will be watching us, will he?'

'You're sure you're all right?'

'Of course I'm all right.'

'You seem to be in a funny sort of mood.'

'Good,' Penelope says. 'I'm glad if I seem that way. We could do with some fun. Let it roll,' she says.

'Oh Pen,' Gwen says and she links her towards the lift. Penelope doesn't object. What's a linking after all? she muses as she presses the lift to go down. While they wait, they smile at a passing middle-aged German couple, or are they Swedish? Well whatever, the couple with the big tomes, their greeting is friendly; that friendly smile is just what they need to start their day. Ah yes, and she finds herself chuckling again.

'I enjoyed our night in,' Gwen says standing on tiptoe to whisper in her ear.

'Bully for you,' Penelope says.

'And you, did you not?' There is a look of impending hurt on Gwen's face.

'Enjoy? Of course,' Penelope says. 'That's what you wanted to hear, isn't it?'

'What?'

'I say and write what people want to hear. That's me, Penelope Eames.'

'I don't understand you, Pen.'

'No labels, remember?'

'Of course not.'

'Well, the labels are shackles for me.'

'Shackles?'

'Yes. I've shaken them off. See? Can you see them? Am I shackled?'

Gwen clucks, at last understanding the charade. 'Ah, I'm glad,' she says and she squeezes Penelope's arm. 'I'm glad for you,

Pen.'

'You're glad for me. I'm glad you're glad for me.'

'Did you have a tipple, Pen?'

'A tipple? Me? Of course I had. Isn't that what you want to hear? A nice little label excuse.'

'A bit early, don't you think?'

'Christ,' Penelope shouts as the door of the lift slides open and a female body lies slumped on its floor, her short red skirt ridden up to her black panties; her legs are twisted under her, her head burrowed into her bloody breast, and there is blood oozing into a pool around her. And both her forefingers, Penelope notices, which are visibly splayed, are missing their nails.

'Oh dearie me,' Gwen says, 'she's dead.'

She hears him screaming. He's having a nightmare. Creepy crawlies are taking over his body. He is clawing at his bare upper torso. He jumps out of the bed. 'Get away. Get the fuck away,' he screams, tearing at the demons inhabiting him.

'They're after me,' he shouts, sweat pumping out of him.

'Who's after you, Dermot?'

He points to the bed.

He prances in and out of the bedroom like a wild animal trying to find his lair.

She gets a towel from the bathroom and runs the cold water tap over it. 'It's all right, Dermot.' She holds him by the arm, leads him to a chair. He makes to get up, but her arm is firm.

'It's all right, Dermot, they've gone.'

'Are you sure?'

'Yes, I'm sure.'

She bathes him with the damp towel, his forehead, his chest. He squirms. 'Tell me, Dermot, about…'

'What?'

'The nightmare you were having.'

'It was real. It was no nightmare.'

'What was it then?'

She knows but she asked anyway. Just in the hope of gaining a further inkling about his condition. 'How much of the stuff have you taken? Will I get a doctor?'

'What stuff?' he says.

Oh, he's back to normal if he can play games. 'Do you take me for a fool, Dermot? You've been taking stuff. You're not "clean". You told me you were "clean"'.

He starts to tremble. She can feel his body palpitate, so defenceless like a little bird's.

'Would you drink a cup of tea or coffee or something?'

'Okay.' He seems to be succumbing. 'Tea,' he says.

She goes to the sink and fills a pot with water.

'What time is it?' he says.

'Three twenty-five.'

'A.m?'

'Of course a.m. Can't you see the darkness?'

He looks dolefully towards the dark balcony with a pearly grey light trying to push its way through.

'What time did you get in? I didn't hear you.'

'Jaysus, it was a horrible experience that. I thought I was going to be eaten alive by -he looks towards the bedroom – those things.'

'There are no things, Dermot. Nothing,' she says soothingly, kneeling in front of him, stroking his arm.

The pot sings. She goes for the teabags, pours two cups.

'We have to talk, Dermot,' she says. 'You know we have to talk. Now is the time,' she says stirring the – she remembers – half tea, half milk; not properly weaned her brother. 'Tell me what's going on in your life, Dermot.'

He sighs, looks out towards the balcony. 'It's all about Will Power. Remember him?'

'I remember him.'

'Dad always said that to me as a kid, and for years I was jealous of this guy that he thought more highly of, it seemed to me, than his own son, or...' he looks towards Penelope... 'his own daughter for that matter.'

'He never thought highly of me. You know that, Dermot.'

'Well, whatever. But this elusive Will Power...' his eyes have become tearful and are pleading to Penelope '... I swear to this day that guy still eludes me.'

'Drink the tea,' she says.

138

He takes the cup. His hand trembles. A drop falls on his boxers. 'Ah fuck.'

'It's all right. It's only a drop,' she says steadying his hand.

'What's that?' he says alarmed and pushing her hand away.

'What?'

'The noise.'

They hear shouting from next door. 'What's that commotion? It's not the cops, is it?'

'Why are you worried about the cops?'

'I'm just asking who it is.'

'Prostitutes,' she says.

'What?'

'One of them was murdered.'

'Fuck sake. Next door?'

'Yes. Gwen and I...'

'Gwen?'

'You met her the first day you arrived, remember?'

'Nosey half pint.'

'We saw her in the lift.'

'Who?'

'The murdered prostitute.'

'Jaysus. That explains how I couldn't... I had to use the stairs.'

'The lift is cordoned off with police tape.'

'So, there are cops.'

'You'll need to be careful with your stuff, Dermot.'

'What stuff? I don't have any stuff. Stop going on about that.'

'Oh, Dermot. It's always the way isn't it?'

'What?' He looks bewildered, stupid almost with his mouth open in a broad O. 'What are you on about?'

'I'm talking about the lack of communication in our family. The way it always was. We're not meant to talk to one another, are we, Dermot? Except in Father's cryptograms.'

'Ah.' He rakes his mop with his fingers. 'Don't...'

'I keep having this dream,' Penelope says. 'I started to write it to try and understand what it means. It's about a blue rope. Hanging in a noose from a tree...'

He jumps up. 'Fuck off,' he shouts. 'Just fuck off.' He prances around the room kicking at the furniture, his hands holding his head as if it is going to burst.

Chapter Twenty Eight

Oh God, she has to hurry. She cannot dwell on things. Tiffany Pringle will be here at two. She would've preferred to have met her in a restaurant or hotel even, but Tiffany said she wanted the interview to take place on her own turf in a natural setting. Natural! What is natural, she wonders, about a high-rise apartment?

At least she has had her hair done and – finally surrendering to Gwen's goading – has had her cuticles pushed back, nails filed to remove ridges and buffed by that gentle Spanish girl who has no English. It was a chance for Penelope to practise her Spanish? Another day perhaps when she will have time, she will be able to concentrate more. She works for Charlie – trabaja, yes. And in the winter when there is not enough employment she goes to work in Málaga at another nail bar. Oh yes. What's sexy about nails? What turns people on about women's nails? Anyway, Charlie was there in a Panama hat – she caught him in the corner of her eye, like an impediment wanting banishment. He was with a few tarty-looking ladies who were queuing to have their nails done and to whom he was mumbling some gruff instructions. He tried to accost Penelope as she was coming out.

'You never called on old Charlie,' he said in that gravelly voice of his.

'I'm in a hurry, Charlie,' she said and she tried to release her hand, but he squeezed, hurting her.

'Charlie, I have an appointment.'

'Ah, an appointment. Maybe you prefer old Bill to old Charlie, what?'

'I haven't an iota what you're talking about, Charlie.'

'An iota,' he says clearly peeved by the word. 'I can give you an iota.'

'Some other time. Okay?'

'That's a promise,' he says.

But it was a threat, she knew as she hurried out the door. And she'd forgotten with all the haste to give a tip to that nice Spanish girl – Charlie had distracted her just at that moment of her rising from her chair. But God, she breathed the welcome air outside. That Charlie, what does he do to one? What emotion does he arouse? Not mere revulsion, no, that is too mild a word; he makes her positively cringe, and she wouldn't be at all surprised if he had a hand in the murder of that prostitute.

How could Gwen see anything redemptive in such a one? Can places of common origin spawn such loyalties irrespective of morality? A puzzle ah, and yet there is Dermot. Would she turn him in? Would she on moral grounds go against her brother? But she must hurry now. She spurs her self onwards through the busy streets of the Saturday shoppers and sea-bound sun worshippers. But she must make haste and not think – not now at least – of Dermot. No. She must look her best, as Sheila forewarned for the occasion. And her tan, despite the interruptions and the high factor creams, was coming along with a nice light golden colour on her arms and around her neck. Would she wear the pearls? The tan would set them off nicely.

But she must hurry. For if she pauses she knows the thoughts will swamp her. The lift is running again. There, you see. She is breathless. There are still some guardias civiles about, but not as many as before. One is posted at the main door, and one inside the vestibule near the lift, observing (she muses) the ups and downs of people. A young guardia smiles at her as she presses the button.

She is about to take her sleek black number from its hanger, when the doorbell rings. God, it couldn't be them already. It's too

142

early, or could it be Dermot? Oh, in what land of demons and coiling snakes did he spend the night? He had gone away miffed because of her dream? And how his language has coarsened in the space of what, how many kilos of ingestion? How many rough lanes of habitation? Oh, what had she done? God, she hasn't time to dwell on these thoughts. She smoothes down her dress, checks herself in the hall mirror and opens the door.

'Gwen.'

'Do you need a hand to tidy up?'

'No, I'm fine honestly,' she says, for she had told Gwen about the impending interview.

'Is it at two they're coming?'

'Yes.' Penelope looks at her watch. 'I'd better get a move on.'

Gwen sniffs, looks around with a foothold jamming the door. 'I'd open a few windows if I were you. There's a Judy Dench in there.'

What does she smell? Penelope wonders beginning herself to sniff, pointing her nose like a divining rod towards the corners of the room.

'When they're taking photographs,' Gwen is saying, 'try to get my picture into it. All right? Wouldn't it be nice to see it in the magazine, like a... little mark you know, something personal.'

Penelope looks towards Gwen's picture of the galloping ponies hanging on the wall. The irony of it. That, as a personal mark.

'I'll try, Gwen. I can't promise. I can't be giving these photographers orders, you know.'

'All right, dearie. But it's a worth a try.'

But is there a pong? There is definitely some smell, she realises, as she closes the front door on Gwen. She slides back the balcony door, opens the bedroom windows letting in the afternoon noise of the same predictable splashing sounds at the pool, like repetitions, she thinks, from the uplifted lid of a sprung music box.

God, is it the stuff? she wonders. Was he smoking crack in his bedroom? And going into Dermot's room, she proceeds to chase the invisible offender around the apartment (if the photographer were to catch her now) with her lemon-scented aerosol spray. Oh, that Dermot, she tuts as she discovers his bed unmade. Typical. She pulls up the bedclothes, checks the wardrobe; it is locked; he must have taken away the key again. She straightens out a few of his toiletries strewn on the bedside locker: a razor – hair invested, cortisone cream for his eczema, something he suffered from since he was a kid – she remembers the flaking pink blotches on his arms and the papery skin on his hands.

Oh, if Dermot would only have sat down and had a long chat, instead of engaging in all this cloak and dagger mystery. He was always jumpy ever since she could remember him, and evasive. She will have it out with him yet if she has to tie him to the bedpost, but... she looks at the bedside clock, Oh my God, she must prepare.

'It was an article of faith,' she hears her voice saying, when Tiffany Pringle asks her what prompted her to write 'such... such...' – and Penelope observes the veins straining in Tiffany's neck as she seeks a word; say it, Penelope wills her, say it or are you of such limited vocabulary that you cannot come up with the word? –'... such raw detail,' Tiffany eventually blurts out. Tiffany is tall and pencil thin (not unlike Topless Jane, except for a quicker perkiness, but is equally boyish with hardly a discernment of breast). Penelope is sitting on the sofa bed in the living room ('Nice place you've got'), the afternoon sun glinting on her hair, making her feel uncomfortable. She shifts an angle, crosses her legs, but there is a problem with her hands – what to do with them? What did she ever do with her hands before, in situations of slight tension in the realm of people? They feel like strange appendages. Ah yes, the Marlboro cigarette she must disdain. She decides to let one hand shake hands with the other, chain them together as it were, and she holds them in that position as the photographer sets up his tripod

'And intent?' Tiffany is saying. She is straddling the tubular chair back to front, using the back to prop up her red and white striped notebook (like a barber's pole, the unwitting symbol of the old surgeons extracting blood). And the chair, the same prop in an unfolding drama only hours before.

Tiffany is stabbing her page with short pungent strokes. Shorthand, Penelope recognises it, the Morse code of journalists.

'I...' God, is she lost for words as well? Mocking is catching. '... I suppose the intent is to portray people as I find them.'

'As you find them?'

'Yes.' God, how boring that sounds. She can see the words etched on Tiffany's heavily powdered face.

'Could you swivel a little sideways?' the photographer says – a peroxide blonde guy with dark eyebrows and a pink shirt with open cuffs, and the tightest and sheerest white cotton pants (almost transparent: one can make out the line of his briefs underneath). How does he bend for those close-up shots? He will burst his seams or, worse, do himself an injury. Now, the camera removed from its tripod, he's in her face, the lens zooming in. 'Yes,' he says and he makes some sign, a coded eyebrow twitch to Tiffany. 'Look natural. That's it. Look away into the horizon, yeah like...' and he catches sight of the picture on the wall '... those horses over there.' Penelope stares at the picture of the ponies. 'That's good. Now I want something different. I want that faraway abstracted writer's look. Should be no trouble to you, eh. That's fine. Good.'

'This is Henri (pronounced in a pseudo-French) by the way,' Tiffany says as an afterthought.

'How do you do?' Penelope says.

'Keep those lips closed,' he says, and then after a few clicks of his camera, 'Charmed I'm sure. Now, Penelope,' and he comes closer again within breathing distance. There is a mint flavour off his breath and a whiff more of a perfume than a cologne. His left hand, with long thin almost skeletal fingers, draws towards her like a reptile. His right hand still holds the camera at shoulder level. 'I'm just raising your hem a little. Yes, that's right. And now you can part your lips, not too much. A little lip gloss to brighten those lips, the colour is fine; just a dab.' And the tube of lip gloss appears as if by a conjuror's sleight of hand, so quick Penelope has no time to object. 'That's it, and uncross your legs.' That hand going through her, like an electric charge, is on her upper torso now. She's afraid to meet his flighty eyes. She keeps looking at the ponies, glad for them now despite her former disavowal. What is he doing? It's like being at a doctor's guessing the codes. She can feel him poking at the top of her dress. Tiffany is not interested in rescuing her, a fellow female. She is writing, not even looking up while this siege is taking place. He's at the top of her dress, pulling at something. He's bending her head forward, his hand brushing against her left breast as if knowing, as if searching out her defects. 'We'll take these things off,' he says. 'You don't mind; they're a trifle passé.' Since when were pearls ever passé? Penelope wonders. 'Let in a bit of light.' He winks. 'A little more décolletage.' Is he talking to himself or to her? 'Yes. Good,' he says without noticing her recoiling. 'Good, good. And now straight at the camera. That's it. This time I want a high voltage smile.'

She bares her teeth.

'Say sex.'

146

'Sex?'

'Good, good.' The screechy pitched tone; he sounds like he's having an orgasm.

'We can continue to work,' Tiffany says eventually looking up, 'while Henri does his thing. So,' says Tiffany turning to a new page, 'you moved over here when?'

'Just a month ago.'

'What made you choose Spain? I mean you could've gone off to… anywhere really.'

'I don't know,' Penelope says. 'I didn't think an awful lot about it at the time. I just knew I wanted to get away out of Ireland that is, and my agent recommended Felicidad.'

'Sheila Flaherty?'

'Yes. She had a place here herself some years ago.'

'Sheila would, wouldn't she?' A muffled snigger to Henri.

A pause for a moment while Tiffany writes.

'You say you wanted to get away from Ireland,' Tiffany says, her ballpoint pen perched thoughtfully at her lips. 'Was there a particular reason?'

What can she say now? She would not like to elaborate, but she knows she has to give these people something to go on.

'Well actually I eh...'

'Yes.'

'I thought I would find inspiration by leaving my own country, you know like Joyce.'

'Joyce? Joyce who?'

Oh God, she is being as presumptuous as the other is being ignorant. 'I mean to get an objective distance on oneself.'

'And did you find this… distance?'

'Yes, I suppose I did.' Stop using the word suppose. Sheila even commented on the overuse of that word when Penelope was interviewed for her first novel. Sheila had listed the word three times, and Gwen also; and even Ramón, he was taking her up on the word *maybe*.

'And before you came over here,' Tiffany says, 'what did you do?'

'What did I do?'

'I mean before your literary success, what...?'

'I did an Arts degree and then I drifted in and out of several jobs?'

'And why was that?'

'I don't know. I never knew exactly what I wanted to do other than to write.'

'And your father, the professor, did he not steer you...?'

'No. He didn't care what I did. But I was always writing,' she continues. 'I mean I had no real interest in any other job, and when my mother died I found myself looking after... well looking after the home a lot of the time.' God yes, should she spell it out? The ironing, the scrubbing, the washing of the lord's dirty underwear and all the time suffering the *put downs*, and time passing and her youth passing and... 'My last job actually was in a museum.'

'A museum?' Tiffany looks towards Henri. 'I don't think we need to go there,' she says, stalling her pen.

'Definitely not a museum,' Henri says.

'So...' Tiffany says looking at Penelope as if she's trying to fathom some strange creature.

'So?'

'The new novel, when do you expect to...?'

'I don't know.'

'What? You've no deadline?'

'Well I...' She was going to say suppose but caught herself in time. 'Within a year they would expect...'

'You're still with Frills and Bloom?'

148

'Yes, I presume so.'

'You don't know?'

'I leave all those things to Sheila. That's what agents are for, isn't it?' She manages a little smile.

'Good, good,' Henri says catching her smile. 'Spontaneous, I like that.' And his camera clicks several times.

'Of course,' Tiffany says and she stabs her page with a flourish. 'And what will it be about? Another hot romance I hope like *Reeking of Roses*?'

'*Smelling of Roses*,' Penelope corrects.

'Oh.' She crosses out the word. 'Oh yes, of course.'

'Actually,' Penelope says, 'it's too early to say.'

Tiffany looks up from her notebook more peeved than puzzled. This interview is not flowing, and her pen is stagnant now, pointing accusingly at Penelope.

'But...'

'Yes?'

'The new book I think will have more to do with the inner workings of people.'

'Inner workings? You mean like engines?' Henri and Tiffany laugh.

'Their inner world,' Penelope persists, 'and how sometimes the outer world is at variance with it. But it will be about people's actions as well. How they act without realising what they're doing in contravention of their logical selves, subliminally almost.'

'Subliminally?' Tiffany pauses, looks away towards the horizon where those ponies are heading, perhaps seeking inspiration from them, or perhaps she is trying to figure out how to spell the word.

'So can we say it's about secrets, then?'

'Perhaps. Yes, secrets,' Penelope says.

'Family secrets?'

149

'Well...'

'And where does the romance come in? I mean at what page does...?'

'I don't know. I'm not sure yet.'

'Okay. Right. Well, it will be set in Spain, that's a given.'

'I don't know. It could be Spain and Ireland.'

'And the title?'

'No title yet.'

Tiffany sighs. There are days like this, the sigh is saying, and the heat is not helping. A drop of sweat surfaces in the hollow of her neck. 'Could I have a glass of water?'

'Of course. There's cool water in the fridge.'

'Don't move,' Henri says, 'I'll get it. Will you have some, Penelope?'

'No, thank you.'

Tiffany takes a tissue which was the little bulge in her trouser pocket and dabs, and the tissue, like blotting paper, soaks up the drop of sweat just at the point when it was about to flow southwards into her blouse.

'What is the temperature?' she says.

'High,' Penelope says.

'Is that your air conditioning?'

The tone is condescending.

'The fan, yes,' and she hears a half-muffled snigger from Henri. 'It's so quaint. Here we are,' he says, careful not to spill the water from the tumblers, which she did manage to buy, and which he had filled a little too much.

'It is about a family,' Penelope says. And Henri smacks his lips, having emptied his tumbler.

'Yes.'

'How people can be abused.'

'Abused?' Tiffany's eyes ignite. She puts her glass down on the low table and quickly resumes writing.

'I mean the damage that families can do to an individual. How they can prevent people from growing, how they can spawn but not necessarily nurture.'

'Spawn?'

'I'm particularly interested in fathers, their role, their power propensity for good or evil, how lives can be altered.'

'Yes.' Tiffany smiles; she's happy with that. 'So that's it at last. That's why you got away,' she says, 'to escape your father.'

'Well, I don't want this to be personal. If we could just stick to it as a motif.'

'Of course,' Tiffany says.

'So, we'll say,' and she starts writing, 'novel in progress.' She looks up. 'Now can you tell me something about all the beautiful people you met over here?'

'Beautiful people? I haven't met many of them.' Oh God, is she going to harp back to her article?

Henri's camera clicks like punctuation points in the conversation, like saying you've been found out now. 'Could we get one on the balcony with you looking out at all the beautiful people?' Henri says.

Penelope is glad to move, to unstick her dress from the sofa.

'That's it, from the rear, just smooth down the dress a bit. We don't want any crinkles and have them crying cellulite now, do we? Look back towards the camera. That's it. Lean forward. Just one more.' Click click. 'Now,' he says to Tiffany, 'could we get her in her bikini?'

'What?' Penelope says. 'You really need that?'

'It is Spain after all,' Tiffany says.

'Do you do this to male writers?'

'Come again?'

'Get them to pose in their swimsuits?'

151

Eyebrows twitch. They don't answer.

'Did Sheila mention it?' Penelope says, 'about the bikini shot?'

'She said it would be fine,' Tiffany says, 'for the magazine, and for your sales.'

'If you got it, flaunt it.' Henri says.

'I'm not a model,' Penelope says. 'I'm a writer.'

'You can be a bit of both,' Tiffany says hurriedly. 'No harm in that. Henri is right. We've got to think image.'

Penelope sighs and moves slowly towards the bedroom.

'You don't mind if I keep going while you change?' Tiffany says.

Penelope doesn't bother answering. Tiffany is going to do what Tiffany wants anyway.

'So have you met any sexy Spaniards over here yet?' Tiffany says through the partly open bedroom door while Penelope changes into her red bikini.

'One or two,' Penelope says non-commitally.

'Sheila is hilarious,' Tiffany says, 'don't you think, the way she puts things? What was it she said? Oh yes, you go for a tan and get a man.'

'Wow,' says Henri, 'I must try that.'

'Sheila said that?' Penelope says.

'She's priceless.'

'Okay,' Henri says as Penelope emerges self consciously tugging at her bikini bottom. 'I want you to lie on the sofa belly down.'

Hesitantly, Penelope moves towards the sofa.

'That's it. Look at me. Good, good. Now I want you to kneel up.'

'What?'

'It's all right,' Tiffany says.

'No, I'm not going to kneel up,' Penelope says.

'Okay,' Henri says, 'we can skip that one.' The eyebrow code is twitching between interviewer and photographer.

'But going back to your family,' Tiffany is saying as she turns another page.

'I'd rather not go into that. I've already told you.'

'Sure.'

'I just felt curtailed, let's say, at home.'

'Irish families,' Tiffany clucks, 'constrain at the best of time. Your mother... when did she die?'

'Seven years ago.'

'Sheila never mentioned it, and your father?'

'I've already told you I don't...'

'No, just a few facts, nothing personal. He is Professor Eames, right, the eminent medical man?'

'Yes.'

'We heard of him. Didn't we, Henri?'

'Oh yes,' says Henri, 'we definitely heard of him.'

'You never felt,' Tiffany says, 'shall we say, overawed by having such a prestigious personage as a father?'

'Maybe I did. What are you writing?' Penelope says alarmed.

'Only what you're saying.'

'He's failing now,' Penelope says, 'so he's not quite as eminent as he used to be.'

'Right.'

'But he refuses to take...'

'Take?'

'Sympathy or help. From anyone.'

'A defiant old bugger, is he? How used he treat you, when you were growing up?'

'Not too well I'm afraid.'

Not too well. Why did she let that slip? She's getting tired. Oh, if only this interview were over.

'Would you care to...?

'Look, I'd rather not, if you don't mind.'

'You mentioned a brother,' Tiffany says determined to continue her prodding. 'Is he younger?'

'Yes. He's here actually in Spain at the moment with me.' God should she have said that? There was no need. 'But only for a while,' she adds as if that will mitigate the revelation.

'What does he do, work at, I mean?'

'You can put on your dressing gown now,' Henri says.

Penelope takes her white bathrobe from the back of a chair, where she had left it draped (in the event of an emergency cover-up being required).

'He's a scientist actually,' she says tying the cord. 'He's over here for a holiday.'

'And what does he think of your writing?'

'Not a lot really. Just women's stuff.'

'Typical men,' Tiffany says. 'Leave them to their cavemen grunts.'

'Ooh, I love cavemen grunts,' Henri interjects.

'You get on well besides that, the two of you I mean?' Tiffany says. 'No sibling rivalry or that sort of thing?'

'No.' What's that got to do with anything? Penelope wonders. What business is it of hers? And looking back at it now, yes, her school results had been every bit as good as Dermot's, but there was nothing made of them.

Tiffany sighs. Negative monosyllables are not good for glossy magazines.

'And your mother, how did she die?'

Penelope blushes. She feels like she has been stabbed, like her entrails are being thrown out on a butcher's table. That old primitive surgeon is ready to dissect her with all his watching acolytes and without even an anaesthetic.

154

'Sorry, Penelope, did you hear me?'

'She just died, that's all.'

'Just died.' She throws a look to Henri.

'What age?'

'Fifty-four or... look I fail to see what my mother or age has got to do with all this.'

Tiffany looks bewildered. 'Does one just die at fifty-four of nothing?'

'Look, I told you.'

'Could it have been a brain haemorrhage?' she says persisting. 'They're common.'

'She died of unhappiness if you must know.'

'Who dies happy?' Henri cheerily pipes in.

Tiffany, perhaps surmising that things could become uncomfortable, snaps her notebook shut, smiles and says, 'Well, I think we have enough now. Thank you, Penelope Eames.'

Chapter Twenty Nine

Ramón phones her. He has some days free, the best part of a week in fact. Would she like to go away? And he speaks in such a sensuous voice, how can she refuse? To allow him the honour (such gallantry, no one ever spoke to her like that before) of showing her something of the real Spain.

'Where? I mean what part?' she says panting, for it is not only the exertion of running to the phone from the shower that has taken her breath away.

'We could head towards Madrid,' he says.

'Oh, but what about Seville?'

'Sevilla,' he says, 'yes we can go there if you must.' 'Oh yes, oh,' and she restrains herself. She mustn't appear too enthusiastic after all it is the law of decorum, the rule of wooing, not to appear over the moon when a handsome man invites a young lady to partake in an adventure, and she as a novelist ought to know better. 'Oh, and let's not forget Salamanca,' she says, 'don't they call it the Oxford of Spain?' 'But more venerable,' he adds. 'You would like it. I have six days. Would you have that much time? We could come back earlier if you wish.'

'Hang on. I'm consulting my diary.' She flicks through some random pages of the manuscript she had been working on (just enough to make a little fluttering noise). She pauses, counts to three. 'Yes, six days should be fine. After all, that interview is over.'

'Ah yes, the interview,' he says, for she had told Ramón also it was forthcoming. 'You must tell me how it went.'

'I'd rather not. I'd rather forget about it, if you don't mind.'

'No problem,' he says. He is so cheerful. His voice, the words, rescuing her from the trough of despond she had floundered in for a couple of days now, not even going to the beach with Gwen, since the interview. She felt so exposed as if she'd been prised open like a jar, and was made to walk around missing her lid; afraid she'd blurt things out to Gwen or anybody about her family, and Dermot of course was tormenting her mind; he hadn't returned since his last outburst. But here is Ramón now with the perfect, almost telepathically delivered antidote – how perspicacious he is – to all those ills. And who knows? but going away with him may even shift that mental block that had plagued her writing too. 'We have something to look forward to now,' he says. Yes. How delightful. She would love to. How wonderful. Of course she would go. 'When?' 'Today'. What? So sudden, so spontaneous. 'Yes, today if you wish.' Oh yes, oh yes, she could hurry, she could pack a few things; it's only for six days after all, but does she know him well enough to trust him? Of course she does. Her small green travel bag should suffice. Oh, but she must iron a few things. What time is it? 'Could we say noon? Could you call for me at noon?'

He picks her up at her apartment in an old Seat cinquecento with little pockets of rust nestling in its red crevices. Character, she thinks affirmingly, yes, tiene carácter.

'Your knees will be striking your mouth,' he says. 'I hope you don't mind?'

'I'm not that tall,' she says. It's to do with him; why did he buy such a small car for such a tall man? 'Is there room in the boot for my bag?' She'd just put in a few things, pyjamas, changes of underwear and a few dresses, a couple of pairs of shorts and a few tops, enough to last six days.

He lifts up the hatchback. There is a little chrome case there already. How neat and orderly, like that of a visiting salesman. He places her bag beside it, taking up the remainder of the sparse room.

157

He adjusts his sunglasses – circular John Lennon style – from the tip of his head onto the bridge of his nose as he prepares to start the engine.

'I never saw you with sunglasses on the beach. They're nice. They suit you.'

'Only for driving,' he says, and she thinks he should have a sports car to go with them or at least a car with a removable hood (rather than a little rectangular aperture that purports to be the sunroof). But there is a quaint innocence in him, she feels, as he drives off the kerb: the lankiness of him. His knees are near his mouth in a squat car reminding her of an adult trying to recapture his childhood in a funfair dodgem. Has he shaved? Apart from the obvious whiff of the ubiquitous Spanish cologne which she finds so appealing, so hygienic, there is no real evidence, for the sun, in its revealing brightness, seems bent on unearthing hidden dark bristles under his chin, a premature five o'clock shadow. But then, she consoles herself, Ramón is dark, sallow. Such men must have to shave at least twice a day, she concludes. Oh, there is a lot to learn about men, about Ramón. She is looking forward to really getting to know him. The little things that make a person.

'So now,' he says, 'vayamos.'

'Yes,' she says rejoicing in the breeze from the sunroof blowing her hair. There was no need to have used that electric hair dryer which she did unthinkingly this morning after her shower, but she was flustered then after Ramón's joyous phone call. Nature, the pleasure of heat, what attracts people, the old especially, to this climate to perpetuate their years. Would her father come here, even for a short stay to visit herself and Dermot in her apartment? Would an ice cube go to hell? Despite everything, she worries how he is faring back there in his own Dundrum defiance. But how could she even for a moment entertain benign thoughts about him?

'Not too uncomfortable?' he says. 'I put the seat back as far as it will go.'

'It's fine,' she says suddenly realising. Had she known this car was so small, they could have hired a spacious convertible. They could have split the cost, but then it would not be the same, would it? Something would be askew. It would not be him: Ramón, sitting there so contentedly beside her (well, one is to presume that by his smile and easy manner that he is content). She was aware she had been hugging her knees which was probably what prompted his enquiry, but she was doing it, not because of being cramped, but because she felt such bliss in the sense of movement; it was like, even if only for a while, feeling that she was leaving her troubles behind.

'This car,' he says, 'I did not buy it for me.'

'Oh.'

'I bought it for my mother. She dreamed of owning a little car to go for drives into the country, to make visits you know to her relatives. It was for her birthday I bought it. My mother always believed there were other worlds you know over the...'

'Horizon?'

'Yes. That's why she wanted the motor car, not just to see her relatives. She was always full of dreams and wishes and anhelos. But she never got to drive it.'

'No?'

'The day I went to collect it was the day she...'

'Oh Ramón, I understand.'

'I never had the heart to sell it.'

'I'm so sorry.'

They travel in a slow, solemn silence for a while in homage as it were to his dead mother. Penelope begins to feel the back of her neck burning, but she is too polite to be so familiar as to ask him to close the sun roof. Instead she unties a pink chiffon kerchief from around the shoulder strap of her handbag – a habit she started in Dublin when she mistook her bag for that of another lady's in Arnotts store – and fastens it around her neck.

He smiles.

She smiles back.

He accelerates to her relief as they come out of town, but still drives cautiously unlike so many macho drivers who speed past. Where are they going in such a mad hurry? It doesn't give the heart a chance to settle. Life was not made for that (despite the kick that speed engenders), not now at least after all that went before in her life, and that's what she likes about her Ramón: he is indifferent to all those macho guys who try to impress their female friends superficially. He does his own thing and goes at his own pace. 'Phew,' she says, 'the speed of that,' as a white convertible scorches past them overloaded with rowdy adolescents. He smiles unperturbed. 'The world will be here after them.' And he recites:

'…*Lo nuestro es sólo mirar que todo pasa*

y es unútil la prisa.'

'It's from a poem, yes?'

'Yes, it means...'

'No, don't tell me; let me try.'

'Our role is to look, to observe, maybe.'

'Observe is good.'

'To observe life as it passes. And what was the other bit? Oh yes, don't tell me, and that haste is useless. Yes?'

'You know a lot of Spanish.'

'I understand more than I can actually express.'

'You got the chance to read some of Unamuno?'

'A little,' she says, 'with the help of a dictionary.'

'And you have understood as I said you would?'

160

'Yes,' she says, 'surprisingly.'

'Nah. Not surprisingly.'

She had genuinely tried to read a little of Unamuno in the interim despite her feeling low. And she thinks yes, Ramón is like Unamuno in his perceiving of life as fundamentally tragic. But in an objective, not a melancholy way.

'He wasn't the least bit depressing,' she hears herself saying. 'He's so erudite. All the languages he quoted from in his quest to fathom the meaning of human existence and his longing for a hereafter.'

Ramón smiles. 'He's fantastic, yes.'

'And the individual,' she adds,

'The yo,' he says.

'Yes. In the universe without frill or adornment, or system, just being.'

'That's the difficult piece,' he says.

'What?'

'To live without system, without adornment. To have faith only in faith itself.'

But Unamuno (and Ramón too) has made her ponder. How to deal with one's destiny honestly. Life is too short for anything less than honesty. And she thinks of her brother's destiny and that of her mother, too late, and even her father (there goes the circle again). But she is or was not responsible for them. How many times does she have to tell herself that? They were and are responsible for their own demise, no matter what. Yes, that is it, and she experiences great relief in herself now in realising such a thing. And life, don't try to romanticise it; what she was doing all along, and that's what they want her to produce in her books: illusions; flavours of the month to provide comfort and solace for fire-side amusement, for chocolate eaters with one eye on the mirror. So make it all bland for word-glancing or page-flicking

161

readers in ready supply of roses without the thorns. Whatever possessed her to agree to a title such as *Smelling of Roses*? *A Standard Romance* was her suggested title, not that it was much better, but at least it didn't have smell in it, and she had followed all the guidelines laid down by her publishers, even to the detail of house style, to produce such a novel. And it must, oh it is imperative (she can hear Sheila's voice), end happily ever after.

She remarks on the huge billboards along the coast road popping up every kilometre or so with pictures of high rise apartments proclaiming: WAKE UP TO THE DREAM.

'Not even in Spanish,' she says, 'those billboards.'

'No,' he says. 'But that is not the dream. That is the phantasm.'

He drives, both of them maintaining a happy silence for a while as they smile out at the sunny day, at the aubrietia blue sky, the extravagant heat that you'd make a meal of if you had it back in Ireland.

'You okay? You are very tranquil.'

'Yes I'm fine.' Tranquil. She thinks of tranquila, the direct translation from the Spanish. Oh, she wants to know more; she feels a hunger to understand more of this huge country and its people. And the whole world, Spanish, sent out in its history from this motherland to the four corners of the globe. Yes, she will master Spanish. She will communicate with the world. She will travel freely, talk like a native through all those countries of South America and Mexico and Cuba. Oh, there are so many places. And she feels such joy as the car turns right at San Roque and heads north for Jerez. The slow-start engine of life is at last running for her.

Gwen had called just before she was leaving all set for the beach. 'I'll leave you to your beau so,' she said. She is good like that, Gwen, not the jealous type. She is just a lonely dear after all, but she persists in defending that Charlie Eliot fellow. 'Poor Charlie,' she said before toddling off. 'One of them foreign tarts blinded him in an eye'.

And Penelope thought, that dead prostitute she saw in the lift, could it have been...?

But it's too ugly a matter to dwell on or to talk about to Ramón now on this glorious day. He is sure, being a local, to know more than her about those unsavoury elements contaminating his town; especially knowing as she does now the circumstances of his mother's death. It makes her more determined to tackle Dermot about the folly of his ways. But she says, addressing her alter ego, don't you dare cloud a sunny day.

'All right?' Ramón smiles at her.

'Fine.'

'She gave us her blessing,' he says.

'Who?'

'My mother.'

'That's good,' Penelope says. It is not strange. It is quite normal, she convinces herself, in the context for Ramón to talk like that.

They stop for lunch in Jerez de la Frontera. She savours delicious tapas of sardines and tortilla with Serrano ham at a bar típico, washed down with a semi sweet amontillado fine sherry which, she said to Ramón, knocked a punch. 'Another idiom to remember,' Ramón says.

'We can look around here or head on to Sevilla. It is for you to say although...' he looks at his watch as they walk in the searing mid-day heat of the Jerez street, 'you can see it's siesta time. She listens. Yes, she can hear the shutters closing. Ghost town, the Spaghetti Western town, the dust rising up. Oh, she should try her hand at writing one of those Westerns, change her name and gender to Hopalong Eames or something and send it off, but it is an outdated genre.

Oh, her mind is wandering again, and good Ramón, honest Ramón, he is so patient. He doesn't force her into conversations like some people she knows, thinking of Gwen in particular. The way she planted words, left them hanging like her gestures towards her or her cryptic reference to Charlie's eye, as if to say you'll come running back to me; I have resources. And Dermot too is reticent with his words, but that is more of a furtiveness. It is important to be accepting of one's silences, to inhabit them and not always wish to shatter their shell. And Tiffany Pringle demanding the title of her work in progress, the absence of which was so bewildering to her, and she wonders why, now that she has time to think in this relaxed little car, what was bewildering about not having a title for a work hardly begun? A title often does not loom clear until the end of a novel. What did she want, that Tiffany one? Something pat, readymade, all plot and cardboard characters, formulaic. And she couldn't even get the title of her fist book right. *Reeking of Roses.* Really!

Her kerchief is chafing as she sinks a fingernail down its side. Anyone would think she had an obsession with her neck the way she is going on. Wasn't there the incident of the pearls also? She hopes Ramón doesn't notice all this fidgeting: a side glance to him, a smile, a forward look. He could consider her – Heaven forbid, one of her father's conditioning terms – a neurotic female. 'We'll move on, so,' she says regretting that she hadn't had a cappuccino or at least a café solo to finish off her meal, for her head is heavy from that sherry; it's beginning to nod despite herself (how many things are despite oneself, she wonders). But Ramón smiles. God, he is easy to get on with: no recrimination or accusation for whatever paltry thing. She almost felt it was the norm, like one's existence was a perpetual argument which had to be justified, accounted for; that's what it was like with her father. But not now, not here with Ramón cruising along in his little chirpy car with its easy salutation to life, making a mockery of worldly vanities. Nevertheless she is conscious of a drowsiness descending on her eyelids; how they grow so heavy.

Noticing her fighting her sleepiness, he says, 'It's okay. You take your siesta. I will wake you up when we are in Sevilla.'

'No. I'm fine.'

'Sure you are.'

And then time for Penelope goes somewhere else.

They are cruising through a town called Dos Hermanas (what a delightful name, thinks Penelope rousing herself) only a few kilometres from Seville.

'I've just thought,' he says, 'we could turn off. It's not far from here. I could show you the caves.'

'Caves?

'Where people live.'

'People live in caves?'

'¿Vale?'

'Vale.'

They turn right into a secondary road for Alcalá de Guadaira and in less that half an hour he is pointing out to her actual dwellings carved out of rock and white-washed walls across their entrances and sporting chimneys and TV aerials. How removed can one get from the fancy villas of the Costa?

'Gitanos, mainly. You didn't believe people could live in caves, did you?'

'No,' she says and she rubs her eyes. Is she still asleep? 'Not in this day and age.'

'Oh but they are comfortable inside. Would you like if I could ask if they could show you inside one?'

'I think we would be imposing… what is that sound?'

'Guitar, of course. Flamenco.'

All the caves seem to echo to the sound, as if an entire orchestra of guitars is playing.

'Very beautiful, yes?'

'Perhaps we should go.'

She is afraid that someone will come out and wave an angry fist at them, justifiably too. She feels like a voyeur intruding on the privacy of people's lives as headscarfed women and barefooted children come and go with their pots and pans. In and out of caves!

And just before Ramón turns the car, they hear the guttural sound of a woman singing.

'Cante jondo,' he says.

'Yes,' she says, 'I've heard the term.'

'It is pure here the sound, like a river at its source.'

The woman is almost shouting to the frenetic strumming of the guitars. She is exhorting, it seems to Penelope, for she cannot understand the words; they are too clipped and harsh-sounding and undoubtedly idiomatic. But she is allowed to imagine, is she not? She is a writer after all – imagine the singer urging her lover on, one would like to think.

'She is rebuking her lover,' Ramón says, 'for spurning her, for being cruel, for leaving her' – and here passion rises in his voice. 'Listen to the sorrow, the agony – what is the word? the crucification.'

'Crucifixion, you mean.'

'Yes, in her voice. It's like that to feel spurned, to feel unloved.'

He speaks so movingly as if he has had first-hand experience of such emotion. Unloved. The sorrow expressed should selfpurge by so expressing, by turning the pain into art,

166

something she has not yet succeeded (if she ever will) in doing with her own unloved past. She wanted to tell him about herself. Where she was coming from; where she wanted to go; what she longed to find in herself. But how could she tell him as yet with such delicate emotion, all-a-flutter like butterfly wings, only beginning to grow inside her now?

Chapter Thirty

He'd just booked one room in Calle de Sepúlveda. She did not object. He asked her of course what she would like, if perhaps she would prefer a room of her own. But there were single beds offering options: together or apart, which seems to be always the way in Spanish pensiones, unlike the no choice take-it-or-leave-it double bed of a guest house which is the norm at home.

But still there is that fear. The night when it will come. How does one ever know someone? There are so many parts to a person. One could spend a lifetime and still not know. Even family, her family anyway, can she say she ever knew them? And she casts a bashful but approving side glance at her handsome beau (chameleon-like, she's adopting Gwen's term now; we slide and slither in and out of each other, it's the way of us humans). But how he waits considerately for her, chastely sitting on the side of the sunflower yellow bed while she finishes her toilet. And rising, when eventually she is ready, and smiling (his face turning to her sun), and yet... and yet carrying all that weightedness as they step out into the Seville streets; how lightly he carries it, not pathologically (that was her father's domain), but in what represents the character of the man, in his tall straight bearing, the weight he talks of is not bearing him down. He possesses a gravitas; yes that's the word, a noble gravitas, like that of a Hamlet or some great tragic figure. But who would believe it, looking at him now, his powerful tanned legs stepping it out in his khaki shorts, as he smiles at the world.

And she will confide in Ramón in due course, she feels it, she knows it, as he, her amphibious lifeguard, leads her carefully across a traffic-strewn intersection.

But to be intimate with him, and she thinks again, with those flutters in her stomach, of the pensión. No matter how her burgeoning feelings towards him are, she will find it strange in revealing herself. That coyness, will it prevent her? When the night comes. And what will he think when he beholds, as inevitably he will, the scar on her left breast? Will he recoil or will it draw him closer? Seeing her breast. Sex and love. When is sex love? ('Make love to the camera. Say sex.' There was no difference in the mouth of Henri). And certainly not that stuff going on in Charlie's, or even that reaching out from Gwen's heartrending loneliness; that was pathos surely.

Love and sex, when do they blend? When do they become one and the same? And she, the erstwhile romantic novelist, virginally poses such a question. And Ramón, he has his own feelings which she must allow for. He has his own upbringing to contend with (is he a Catholic for example, as so many Spaniards and Irish appear today in a lapsed sort of way? His faith in faith alone. Or is his being drawn towards his mother's cemetery purely out of filial love?). But there is nothing lapsed about Ramón, she can feel it in his firm grip as they cross the street, his strength, his passionate sincerity shining through that august mind. And sexually and otherwise, she will have to take on board his views on such matters. After all she is being selfish, just looking at everything from her own womanly angle.

Still, she wonders, what images, fantasies, do men have of women? And specifically what fantasy (if any) does Ramón carry of her? Does he buy Kellogg's corn flakes? Hardly. Cornflakes are not the thing over here. And what image does she carry of him? He will be caring, sensitive, gentle. Oh stop it; she is returning to the romantic novelist phase, that she was criticising only moments ago. God, how is she ever going to write again with such contradictory oscillations going on in her head? Oh Penelope, who would think that your modest, taciturn exterior belies such an introverted garrulousness?

169

Ramón – she can't resist herself speculating, no matter what – is he as benign on the interior as that outward show. Her pyjamas, she realises startlingly, the three pairs she brought with her, that she is so used to wearing, she wasn't thinking, she just threw them into her travel bag. Will he find them off-putting, too masculine perhaps? She should have included her white cotton nightdress also. But it was all so rushed in the leave-taking as she remembers. He had quite stolen her breath away.

But spontaneity – she quickens her pace, 'You are in a hurry,' he says keeping in step with her – should be the order of the day.

And of the night.

Chapter Thirty One

He is perusing poetry books in the bookshop, seductive, sleek tomes of poesía. In contrast, her eye is corralled by the almost billboard size lettering of *Cómo Escribir Un Blockbuster*.

She picks up the book. Does she have any choice? With its psychedelic cover screaming at one for attention. She flicks through the pages. Even in Spanish, she reflects, they are all the same, these books, the same clichés, the ingredients for success for the bestseller, for the blockbuster, what you must stir into the cooking pot, how to write Capítulos Proactivos. She can read the words; it's the same jargon, how to begin the genre – that accursed word. Guía Definitiva. 'We (the gurus, the Gods of creation) will give you the tools, the technique to show and not to tell.' She laughs. He looks up from his poetry book towards her, smiles. How to get noticed by a literary agent. How to avoid all the pitfalls. The tome is heavy (she gauges it), a hardback too, expecting to sell a lot. The how-to-write a bestseller book evolving before her eyes as other people pick up copies. Who are they, these budding writers, middleaged women and greyhaired men in their humility and wrinkled innocence? Ah yes, for the young don't need to know; they can rely on their looks or their celebrity to guarantee sales. Their nails, she thinks, and she looks at a photograph of a blowsy author flaunting her long scarlet nails, as if giving off a sexual message. How important nails are. And she regards her own cuticles, the cerise paint showing signs of wear. And she wonders where does she fit now, Penelope Eames, into this scheme of things? Is there a scheme, a system? - Unamuno did not think so. But here she is in a Seville bookshop on a street whose name she does not know, and she is a witness to this attention-seeking tome as it were. It evolves by its very making into a bestseller in its own right. She smiles rakishly: the greyhaired gentleman is surreptitiously writing notes from it into a small black notebook, the grey goatee beard of the hidalgo hanging from his chin – if he wore a cloak he would transport one back centuries, to novels of dark intrigue. The middle-aged woman, plump with the spectacles and the navy dress, is making her way to the cash desk supporting the volume like it is a huge brick under her oxter as she cools her face with a fan that, fast as a flickknife, opens and shuts. And it could happen, that phenomenon, as another buyer appears on the queue, by the sheer weight and arrogance of its content, that a how-to-write book could outsell a book itself. How to avoid all the pitfalls. Ah yes, if only... the pitfalls. A little shudder of anxiety unhinges her until a hand, his hand, is felt warm and comforting on her shoulder.

'Shall we go to the Gardens of María Luisa now?' he says.

'Yes please,' she says and she knows her tone is that of one being rescued from oneself.

Chapter Thirty Two

The overpowering heat, as they enter the Gardens, fans out from its oppressiveness (could the sun be patriarchal? she wonders) contained by city walls.

The shade is welcomed by Penelope of palm and orange trees. Oh, how she'd have loved to smell the orange blossom, but notwithstanding, 'I'd love to come here in April,' she says, 'to see all the fairs and processions.'

'No, you would not,' he says squeezing her hand.

'No?' She laughs. 'Why do you say that?'

'You would not like it,' he says, 'because those things, all those fancy ceremonies, it is just the havenots... that is the word, yes?'

'Yes, I suppose but...' she says unsure what he is driving at.

'The havenots,' he repeats, 'looking up at those who have. It is a chance for the rich to show off all their finery. You know they take greater care of their horses than they do of their servants.'

'Surely not all.'

She looks at him silently, amazed at this sudden bitterness in his tone.

'All those so-called nobles. What a misuse of a word.' He sighs. 'Yes, she was treated like that.'

'Your mother?'

'Ah Sevilla,' he says, 'spelled servile for mi madre.'

She waits for him to elaborate but nothing is forthcoming. They pass silently by Fuente de las Ranas, past elms and Mediterranean pines and hidden bowers yes, for real lovers' trysts, she thinks, unlike those holes for the profligates on Charlie Eliot's estate.

'Look at that beautiful statue,' she exclaims partly to break the silence.

'It's of Bécquer,' he says.

173

'The nineteenth-century poet.' She remembers reading something about him.

'My favourite poet,' he says. 'He was born so poor.'

Is it the man and his condition, she wonders, or his poetry that Ramón likes?

It is just the white grey torso that is revealed of Bécquer, as if the rest of him is sunken into stone, a bearded and curly head astride a garlanded plinth, guarded by an angel under whom three female figures are seated.

'Let me show you the three figures,' he says. They approach the statue under its shady bower.

'What a wonderful place,' she says welcoming the relative coolness afforded by the shade.

'He is like your English Keats.'

'Not mine.'

'But romantic.'

'That word,' she says.

'You have problems with that word?'

'Only in its misapplications.'

'Have I misapplied it?'

She smiles. 'Oh no, not you, Ramón.'

'Tragic,' he says referring back to the poet, 'dying so young, all for love.'

All for love. She sighs, looking up, trying to study the visage of the poet for hidden secrets of his impassioned life. But he looks stoical, passive with nothing, no expression in his gaze; like a Roman emperor with hollows for eyes. But his cast is downward; at least there is that.

'Those three figures,' Ramón says, 'what they represent.'

She examines the three girls sitting at the base of the plinth, underneath the angel whose outstretched wings fend off evil.

'Full love,' he says. You see the way the faces are. Dreamed love, the upward look, the hand on the breast. And the downcast one which is ...' He pauses. Does he want her to guess?

'Lost Love. Of course,' she says.

'So,' he says.

'So?'

'Which is yours? Choose the lady.'

'Not lost love anyway,' she says standing up on one of the steps of the plinth to study the downcast look of the girl. It's like she has expired, given up the ghost, all hope gone, the girl with the curls (did they all curl their hair in those days?) and the arms crossed protectively (too late for virtue now) over her wide flowing dress.

'No, definitely not her,' and then philosophically she adds, 'for I never had love to lose.' God, is she aware what she has just blurted out? It's like her inner and outer worlds are colliding now here with Ramón. Or could it be that some of that strong sherry is still addling her brain?

'You never knew love?' he says. He looks concerned, a wrinkling in his brow. 'How is it possible? How could someone never have known love?'

'It's not impossible,' she says matter-of-factly, 'if you come from a family like mine.'

'Your family,' he says, 'they were not loving?'

'Not really. But I will tell you about that some other time. If you will allow me.'

'Allow you? Of course I will allow you. I will be privileged.'

Now she has done it. Oh no, she feels she's sinking into that familial mire once more. 'But for now I choose dreamed love,' she says snappily (snapping shut the inner demons), and she turns and gazes into Ramón's compassionate eyes. 'In the hope that it will become full love,' she adds.

'But not full yet?' he says.

175

'No, not yet. Not yet full.' She presses his hand. 'But...'
'Yes?'
'But... filling.'

She trembles as his fingers gently open the white bone buttons of her pyjama top. The first one yields. The second one is recalcitrant; the hole is too small perhaps, too tight for the round disk. Maybe she should help him; join her fingers to his. But no. It would make her appear too eager, brazen, unfeminine. The button yields. What had he said? That she was the flower in the desert of his life. He has addressed her, and now he is undressing her. But how can she play with words at a time like... this? When the night is warm and balmy and the stars outside are twinkling like a Greek chorus to the moon? It is, she knows, to fight the modesty in herself, eyes cast down, like that statue of love lost, afraid to hold his gaze as he slides her top from her shoulders.

He sees the scar. She feels his stare burning into it.

'The wound,' he says.

'It's nothing,' she says. 'It was something, but not any more.'

Was she ever more exposed? His full frontal gaze, but she realises as she forces her eyes upwards to meet his, that his look is one of solicitude.

He kisses her and she feels, enfolded in his arms, as one frozen all her life, at last beginning to thaw.

Chapter Thirty Four

'The moment I speak of,' he says stirring morning coffee in a café near the Alcázar, 'is when you see crystal clear.'

She feels the frisson still there from the night previous as she listens to the words he is speaking, as if he had just left off – a good example of the imperfect tense in Spanish, what I was doing when something interrupted (God, was their lovemaking an interruption?) mid-sentence like that medieval lecturing monk she read of who was abducted by vagabonds in the middle of his lecture, and returned years later with 'as I was saying'. Life really is continuity, or should be. Even the jolts have to have a pattern somewhere, but no, that would be system again. Why are we always seeking it? Afraid of plunging into the great gaping chaos otherwise.

But she must concentrate on what her lover (yes her own, her very own real and dear lover) is saying. How intimate she feels with him now as he found her not wanting, accepting her, and she him. Intimacy breeding familiarity: the curled toe, the position of a hair, the scar, and familiarity breeds... love, yes, knowing someone, feeling as she does now, so close physically (she can touch him wherever, whenever and he, yes, he can touch her in those intimate parts, and spiritually, yes; it is that which makes the sexual other than a mere flesh transaction; she is one with him too). Knowing and not being ashamed, yes.

There is a bounce not only in her hair, which she has just shampooed with the flounce shampoo, but in her whole self. And his weighted words – listen to them, pay attention, she chides herself, for she had been in her own reverie (as we all are, she supposes, sometimes) taking the words in more for their rhythm and lilt than for their meaning. How accustomed one can become to the words of another. Like a breath or an idling engine.

'The limitation of life,' he is saying, 'when you see the opportunities that have gone begging. You can say that, gone begging?'

'Gone a-begging.'

'Gone a-begging. When you know, you have gone past the stage of opportunity or wherever, like my mother perhaps.'

'Yes.'

'You know because of your circumstances you will never, never reach that stage, that you will remain always downtrodden.'

That word downtrodden has struck home and she concurs whisperingly as if they are conspiring together in some anti-patriarchal revolt.

'That was my mother too.'

'They had the capacity to grieve for lost opportunities.'

'Yes.'

'But when does it occur, this moment, when it is not longer bearable? The truth of things is no longer bearable and we cannot disguise it in fine clothes. The moment when...'

'Don't say it, please.' She seals his lips with the long nail of her forefinger.

'I'm sorry, have I...?'

'We should not live in our parents' shadows.'

'Yes, you are right, but how do you escape the shadow?'

'I don't know. I don't think I can ever say I knew my mother. Or did she even know herself? She was not allowed – isn't that a terrible thing to do to somebody, to prevent them from being themselves? Her own personality was stifled by him. It's funny; it's only now that things are, as you say, crystal clear. Before that I was too young to work out such matters. I was drowning in my father's obfuscations.'

'Obfuscations?'

'Yes. Words could be used to justify anything, and my mother and I, we were made to feel inferior by his constant verbal barrage. Yes, the same thing he did with her, he was trying to do with me. It's crystal clear. You have made it clear for me.'

'I have?'

'Oh yes, Ramón, you.'

She kisses him, a quick peck of affection on his left cheek.

'But you are young and you are free now.'

'I came away.' How did she leave that Dundrum home? The circumstances? Where was the boiling point? Did she walk out, slam the door? No, that was Dermot's modus operandi. The last rainy night in Dublin was a frizzle-out, not a blow-out, an accumulation of disgruntlements launching her onwards, as she tried to escape the feeling of a life being frittered away. She just had to go. She could take no more. It was an inevitability rather than a cataclysm. And her father, doddery and all as he was, had taken himself off to his study. He was the one who had closed the door on her. She turned away, suitcase in hand, saying, 'Goodbye, Daddy,' to a closed door.

She sighs.

'What is it?' he says anxiously.

'The finding and freeing of oneself, is it ever attained?'

'But why, why do you say that?'

'My brother,' she says.

'Your brother?'

'Yes, my younger brother, my only brother, he has arrived in Spain.'

'Is that not good?'

'Good?' She looks towards the sky. 'He has brought with him the wind and the rain.'

180

'All that land,' he says seeing her gazing out at the vast arid tracts, 'owned by the few, worked by the many. My mother...'

'She was one?'

'They made her work on her knees.'

She pictures it: his mother in the sable black on her knees, a peon with a venerable lineage working the fields (where did it all go wrong?); gathering the grapes and the olives under a blazing sun. Oh, she is feeling guilty. Those olives, why did she stuff her face with them in the restaurant on that first date?

'From all the work in the fields?'

'Oh no, not in the fields. On the floors of the rich, cleaning their cesspools,' he says bitterly. 'Even with walking she had difficulty later. That's another reason why she longed for a car.' And gravely he adds, 'That's why she could not run away from her assassin.'

'Oh, Ramón.' What can she say? – her tone is saying it – to show how she feels for him? Her hand reaches out, hovers, unsure what part of him to touch as he drives. She elects to rest it platonically on his shoulder.

'But she had a dream for me,' he says, 'that did come true, to educate her boy. That's why she used to send me to Dublin with all those rich kids. How she toiled – he measures the word – toiled yes, and saved to do that. I remember all the students buying their Nike runners and Irish smoked salmon and spending, spending; they were like locusts in all the big department stores of Dublin. I used to carry a Nike runner box around the streets with nothing inside it. Just to give the impression you know...'

'If I'd only known you then... we could've...' She wants to be upbeat, to cheer him up, to say she could have rescued him from those rich kids.

'Yes.' He smiles. 'Perhaps.'

Perhaps? Perhaps what? What is his wavelength? What is he thinking? What would they have done in Dublin had they met? They would have been too young to engage in anything other than a short-lived teenage affair at the most.

'But would we have had the wisdom then?' she says.

'You think we have the wisdom now?'

'I don't know. But you...' He looks at her. It is a quiet part of the road now. No other cars, just them.

'Me?'

'You have come to my country, and you are the writer. It is a great calling.'

'Oh Ramón, spare me. I am just... a silly lady novelist.' She remembers the term; she had come across it somewhere, yes, in an article written by George Eliot.

'No,' he says, 'not silly. You are the recorder of the truth.'

Those words of his, they may carry weight (his weightedness) in Spanish, and the few South American novels she has read would seem to bear it out, or even in the works of some of those eastern European artists struggling under oppressive regimes. But in English in translation they sound so over the top for this day and age, haughty and antiquated. But Ramón is not haughty. They are just the words entrapping him, and she thinks, it is his conditioning, his ideological weaning.

'You have a power.'

'That's a load of tosh.' She stretches, fighting back a yawn. 'What power do I have? I have as much power as an emery board or a box of chocolates.'

'No. It is true. For you to lie...'

'Who said I would lie?'

'But if you were to lie, it would be a great pecado.'

'Sin? Ha. Sure fiction is itself a lie, Ramón, don't you know that?'

'Not a lie, a distortion perhaps, but only in order to get at the real truth of things. People, thousands of people, will be influenced by your words.'

'Do you really believe that?'

'Of course I believe that,' he says. Teacher and writer, we are both of noble professions. Noble,' he repeats, 'in its true meaning, and,' he adds venomously, 'not like those rich, good-for-nothing hidalgos with their inherited titles. Noble, yes, making us blessed and cursed at the same time.'

'God, Ramón, if I didn't see you and hear you in the flesh, I would've said you were an old, old man.'

'An only child is born old,' he says.

'Oh, come on.'

'No, it's true. Who has he got to keep him young?'

'And you really believe that, don't you, about the teacher and the writer I mean?'

'Sí, señorita.'

'But do you teach your pupils just sadness. Is that all?'

'Oh no, it is not sadness. I teach them to walk humbly.'

God, that is exactly the phrase, the concept that had eluded her. If only her father had...

'But also,' he is saying, 'I teach them passion, to have passion for things.' He sighs. 'It is difficult. You can't talk about it. You have somehow to get them to live it, set them on fire. It is something to be seized like the horns of el toro, something that would be... emasculated, you can say that? by the intellect.'

'Oh, but Ramón, the poor old intellect,' she says derisively, 'it takes a terrible battering.'

'But passion,' he says.

'Yes, passion I'll not deny, but like a candle it goes out and

183

you can't rely on it. What we need is steadiness and insight to get us through.'

'Get us through?'

'Comprehend the world. Comprender, you know?'

'Of course.' He turns the handle of the window, drawing the window down fully. He sighs.

'How do you think or reach your views on things?' Penelope says rolling her thoughts into words. 'Your love of Unamuno. Your theory of weightedness for example, was arrived at by the intellect. The intellect is our antenna on the world.'

Oh God, why is she saying these things? A shudder – she is sounding like her father, with his fondness for the polysyllabic (except when being found out). How could she do such a thing? She will frighten him away. But what does she really want to say?

'But...' he says.

'I don't by that mean...' she says mustering a final captured thought, like a debater saying, let me finish... 'an arrogant intellect.' Yes, she is determined to clarify this as the image of her father looms before her. 'What I mean, and forgive me for going on about it, but what I mean is, to possess an enquiring mind is surely something not to be denigrated. That sort of intellect, I could not imagine myself ever being without it.'

'Perhaps you're right,' he says finally ceding to her, 'once you're not crippled by it as sometimes I feel I am.'

'I don't think you're crippled,' she says.

He slows down. The thought is taking over the controls; he has moved into the slow lane; cars and trucks zip by on the fast lane. 'It is difficult, this driving and arguing.'

'Arguing?'

What is wrong? Has she upset him? Oh God, that was not her intention.

'Ramón, I...'

'Presenting the contrary view, that distracts the mind.'

'Do you want to stop at a café somewhere?' she says, for he looks flustered and quite out of breath, like a runner who has run a long distance.

'No, I'm okay now,' he says.

'But it's not bad, arguing I mean...' Penelope says.

'Oh no, not bad but demanding. You are a demanding woman, Señorita Eames. Remember it is only little children who talk back to me.'

God, there is such an innocence about him. Compared to him she's worldly-wise. Who would have thought it, seeing him in all his physicality on the beach?

'Am I, Ramón?' Her voice is softer, trying to capture a winsomeness. 'You really think I'm demanding?'

He pulls into a lay-by, stops the car.

What is the matter? Is he becoming overwrought again?

'The oil light has come on,' he says. 'I have to top it.'

'Top it up.'

'Yes.'

'Is it okay?'

'It burns a little. I have to keep an eye on it.'

She sits waiting for him, feeling the air stealing like danger in from the open door. She is too polite to close it or to shout to him to close it, but she knows it will only be a temporary discomfort. Still, the feeling is there, the cold consciousness of his absence. But soon he's back and with, 'That's okay now', he is pulling out again onto the open road.

'Some of those children that I teach,' he says, and she sees his knuckles whitening as he grasps the gears, 'those...'

'Expats.'

'Yes. They are different. Sometimes when their parents come to see me, they are giving orders, and some of their children, they

185

don't return to school for days on end. You can say on end?'

'Yes.'

'So it is very difficult for them to have continuity. They have no loyalty to their adoptive country. It is the other side of the coin. That is the idiom, yes. You see symptoms.'

'Symptoms?'

'Of the drugs. You recognise the children of the addicts. They are always fidgeting, or staring out the window. You can see their mood swings, their withdrawals from the other children, their anger at the world their... how you say...?'

'Tantrums.'

'Yes. But they are victims. They are the innocents, and yet they have all the symptoms of the adult addicts. Of their parents, can you believe it, what these parents have inflicted on their children? All the pain yes, without experiencing any of the pleasure.'

'I can believe it,' Penelope says. With intensity she can believe it.

'It's like they're wondering all the time when the other children are singing or rhyming off their tables, wondering where they are and what they're doing here.'

They drive in silence for a while, heading north towards Madrid and Salamanca, and she looks out with new eyes at theses strange latifundios, receding now in mystification.

Ramón is talkative now, excited almost. He will show her Calle de O'Donnell. They will have lunch there. How will she like that, eating lunch on an Irish street in the heart of Madrid? The capital city. De Madrid al cielo. She has heard that phrase, she tells him: from Madrid to the heavens. 'It is a load of nonsense,' he says, 'like see Rome and die.' He will bring her to The Valley of the Fallen which has a huge cross to commemorate all the dead on both sides in the Civil War. He remembers the last time he was there: he had brought the children on a school trip. He met an old woman weeping. Had she lost her husband or a relative in the War? he asked. '"No," she said, "no, señor. I have lost a son in the construction of this accursed cross." So you see, even memorials are not without blame.'

But they'll move on to Salamanca; he has it all planned: they will stay the night in a pensión he has booked (because Salamanca is a popular place at this time of year) near the cobbled square of Plaza Mayor, and he will show her the college that was once the Irish college and the cemetery where his mother perhaps could have been buried if it hadn't been so far away, with a Gaelic script adorning her grave.

The cemetery yes, with the Gaelic names printed on their tombstones, she remembers from her history. Yes, the Irish priests who studied there during the Penal times. And he will show her his ancestor's name Ó Dónaill with the accent marks just like in Spanish. 'Why does English have no accent marks?' he asks. 'I have often wondered.'

'I don't know. I never thought about it before.'

'It's like saying they are a passionless people.'

'Passionless?'

'Yes. They put no stress or emphasis anywhere in their language. It is a yoke.'

'A joke.'

'Yes,' he says. 'Let me tell you a funny story that happened in Ireland. It concerns a modismo, an idiom you know. We were on a boat on the Shannon, the river, yes, and one student was very interested in the boats and he asked the boatman to let him take the... the...'

'Helm?'

'Exactly. We were navigating along and the teacher told us that we were behind the time, that the bus was waiting and he told the student to step on the gas. And the student, he looked so confused I remember, and he said, "But sir, where is the gas?"'

Her mobile phone rings, blasting through their laughter. 'Excuse me.'

He drives silently now, worriedly as he catches the words of argument, real argument and the paling of Penelope's face.

She puts away the phone, reaches for her handbag and, with trembling fingers, takes out a Marlboro cigarette.

'Are you all right?'

She doesn't answer. She presses in the car lighter.

'What is it, Penelope? What is wrong?'

'I have to go back. I'm sorry. The weather has changed,' she says sucking on her cigarette. 'There is going to be wind and rain.'

Chapter Thirty Six

'There wasn't enough for Charlie.'

'What?'

'After the cop seizure. You heard about that?'

'Yes, but what's that got to do...?'

'Cheap shit to keep Charlie happy.'

'So it was Charlie, then?

'What?'

'The person you had to go and see.'

'They were short after the raid, but Charlie, that bollox, the connoisseur, he knew what I was up to.'

'What were you up to, Dermot?'

'He copped it immediately. Fuck him anyway. Only for him...'

He pushes back his fringe, revealing the sweat ready to drip off his forehead.

'Tell me, Dermot.'

'Have you a tissue or something?'

She gets him a tissue from a box on the kitchen workshop.

'Maybe you'd like a Toblerone as well?' she says unsympathetically.

He mops his forehead. 'Cut it out, sis.'

'No, I won't cut it out. You bring me back to tell me all this. Do you know where I was that time you phoned? Have you any idea?'

He doesn't answer. He slouches towards the balcony.

'Have you?' she repeats with a rising inflection.

'No.'

'I'll tell you where I was, Dermot, not that you're interested in me or my welfare. I was trying to make a life for myself, you understand. I was making a stab for the first time in my life at happiness. But you had to butt in, didn't you?'

'So that's it,' he says making towards the front door.

'Wait,' she says, 'I didn't mean that, Dermot. But I don't know what you're looking for. What do you want me to do? What do you expect of me?'

'Charlie,' he says, 'he's given me twenty-four hours.'

'What? What are you talking about?'

'I have to buy stuff for him.'

'Ha, twenty-four hours,' she says sarcastically. 'How original. How theatrical.'

'Cut it out.'

'I won't cut it out.'

'I'm in serious shit.'

Shit. That word. She remembers at the party, Charlie in the shrubbery saying it better be good. 'You told Charlie you'd good shit.'

'I didn't think that bollox would know the difference.'

'You're a liar, Dermot. You told me you were *clean*.'

He presses his palms hard against the sides of his temple.

'I'm going to give you money,' she says getting her handbag from the table, 'this time, Dermot, but I'm not going to help you any more.'

'Fuck you.'

'Dermot.'

'No. Fuck you,' he says again, slamming the door after him.

Chapter Thirty Seven

Night finds them walking along the beach of Felicidad past the folddup sunbeds and sheets of tarpaulin covers blowing in the wind, the sand dark and damp under their feet. She is walking in her bare feet, carrying her sandals and holding a cigarette in the same hand. She is leaning into him, his right arm around her waist. Their heads are downcast.

'I am so sorry, Ramón. And you had booked the pensión in Salamanca.'

'Forget about that.'

'He just stormed out.'

A gibbous moon sheds enough light to show the water, the inky colour of it.

'I was going to give him the money,' she is saying, 'I offered it to him, but he just...' She refrains from using Dermot's F word... 'he just slammed the door. Typical. Oh so easily insulted, so bloody moody, Dermot as always. I just told him, Ramón,' and she looks up to gauge her lover's level of credulity in his half-shadowed face, 'that I would not give him money any more after this. Don't people have the right, Ramón, to live their own lives? Don't they?'

'Of course they do.'

The waves crash like cannon roar, spending themselves in foamy bubbles near their feet. She feels the shifting sand and the ebbing water between her toes.

'And when I said that would be the last time I'd help him, that's when he...'

'Shh.' He crosses a finger on his lips.

'What?' Does he want to silence her? Does he not want to know about Dermot?

'Listen.'

They listen for a moment.

'What is it, Ramón?'

'I heard something.'

'Where?'

'Out there, in the sea. A sound of splashing.'

'It's just the waves.'

'No,' he says, 'I know the waves.'

He releases his arm from her, removing the warm feeling, leaving her to sense the cool sea breeze at the small of her back. He walks away down the beach.

'Ramón, where are you going?'

He doesn't answer but quickens his pace into a half run before wading into the sea.

She keeps him in her line of vision until the sea swallows his lower limbs and he is just a torso now, like Bécquer's statue, perched on the pitchy surface.

'Ramón.'

He disappears into the blackness.

She looks around; there is no one, not one person, no young lovers with secret trysts groping each other around the boats or lying entwined on a purloined sunbed. No one to call on. Should she stay or seek help? Should she run to the police station which is a good kilometre away? A lot could happen in that space of time. She calls again. This time even the water doesn't reply. It too seems to have gone silent as if there is some intrigue (could it be possible? she wonders) between man and cosmos, as the moon holds back the waves.

Then, after what seems like an infinity, but she knows is just matter of minutes, she hears groaning from the depths. There are splashing sounds and in the moonlight she sees him emerge, slowly pushing his strong weighted thighs from the bloating of his jeans against the weight of water, carrying in his arms the body of a man.

'Dermot. Oh God,' she exclaims on recognising her brother.

Ramón still does not speak, so intent is he, like a priest in his ablutions – the analogy fleetingly crosses Penelope's mind – on the ceremony he is enacting. She understands, every moment could be a matter of life or death. Is it already too late?

'Oh, Ramón, is he gone? Is he... dead?'

Again Ramón refuses to speak, but gently lays Dermot down on the wet sand, loosens his collar, pushes back his head and flicks with his forefinger bits of seaweed from the corners of his lips; then pinching his nostrils he breathes into his open mouth, thumping his chest alternatingly. How many breaths, how many thumps, she's lost count. They wait. Nothing. No response. Ramón repeats the procedure. Again the wait. 'Oh Ramón.' Suddenly what seems like half an ocean spurts from Dermot's mouth and the chest, the puny chest like a little machine starting up, commences to heave, too fast, catching the breath, and now spluttering more slowly, up and down.

'Oh Dermot,' Penelope cries as Ramón turns her brother on his side. What she wants to say is what a foolish person he is, but she is afraid of what he might do, what he might attempt to do again. Oh, why did she argue with him about the money? Why did she say it would be the last time? Why did she give that finality to one like Dermot, so brittle?

'I think he'll be all right now.' Ramón stands up, speaking at last.

Dermot squirms from the gaze as if a bright light is strobing him, rather than the faint luminosity of the moon.

'Fuck off, you,' he shouts twisting and turning on the sand like a caught fish, and trying to hide his face with his hands. 'What...' and he grasps for breath... 'gave you the right to interfere?'

193

'Ramón is a lifeguard, Dermot,' Penelope says.

'Lifeguard.' He spits into the darkness, his hands still covering his eyes. 'Who wants a lifeguard? He thinks he's done something great. He's just added to the continuation of the problem.'

'Dermot, we can talk about it. We can solve it together, no matter how bad the problem is, we can...'

'Leave me alone.'

He raises himself unsteadily on to his feet and, coughing and spluttering, stumbles away from them.

'Dermot, where are you going?'

Ignoring her, he wanders up the beach, the sounds of him fading, and out of the light of the moon.

'Dermot,' she shouts, 'we can solve this.' But as she makes to run after him, Ramón's hand gently restrains her.

'You can only save a life once,' he says.

Chapter Thirty Eight

'I don't even have his mobile number,' she says as back in her apartment she searches frantically through Dermot's things. 'It was always blocked any time he phoned me.'

'Don't go after him,' Ramón says. He is almost annoyed by her antics; she can see by his expression – the frown and deep inhalation, but never spoken; all those hidden things in people, and she is the writer and she never captured those things before, those shades of difference. What good is it? What good is writing if we don't capture the unspoken language of people? But this is not the time to dwell on such matters. You don't just abandon a brother who is crying out in need. How could she... how could she turn her back? 'This is real flesh and blood, we're talking here, Ramón,' she says, 'not one of your metaphors.' 'My metaphors?' Yes, and there is an edge in her tone which she hadn't really meant, but there it is, intimating their first friction. 'I can't just... not after... I feel responsible, no matter what.'

'No matter what,' he says in a gentle mimicry. 'I tell you not to go and you go. He is not your brother.'

'He is my brother.'

'Please don't think he is your brother.'

'What do you mean he is not my brother?'

'Not any more.'

'I'm sorry, Ramón, but I have to go.'

All in a flurry she had parted from him. Rude, rude. Was she... was she rude to close the door on him so... so abruptly, to leave him in the lurch like that? But what else could she do?

She searches Dermot's room turning up things, tossing things. She ransacks the wardrobe, prising with a kitchen knife the weak lock, accessing Dermot's frayed handled bag, a sticky zip opening to a few empty Toblerone boxes, a hydraulic pump, a scales and his red tin of talcum powder. But wait, what's this peeping out from under the bottom flap? A soiled white envelope.

Tremulously, her nails unstick the gum-worn overlap to reveal a letter in her mother's familiar slanted handwriting:

To my darlings, Penelope and Dermot,

Please forgive me. Please believe that I always loved you, that I wanted to love you so much. More than anything in my worthless life. To make both of you strong in the world. To go out there and be strong. That was my fervent wish. There were so many things that I wanted, that I had planned to do for you both. I was so proud of you, Dermot. How you excelled in school. You must have got all that from him (what would you have got from me anyway?). Oh, I hope you go far and prosper. And you, Penelope, with your writing and your imagination – wherever it came from, it is your own. Use it. Although I fear for you that you may learn too many of life's secrets. But your father is right about me, as he always is; his words last night – something... something happened, like a shattering; his final shot struck home: I am a burden to you all.

I'm so sorry,
Mam.

There is a smudge over the word love: a dried tear? She remembers when she got the emergency call, her blinkered return from London, yes. Her mother – she had not been well when Penelope had left, but was suffering nothing more than her usual complaints – was laid out in her bed and... the sheet was covering her right up to her chin and... so sudden, so fast she was whisked away.

But what was Dermot doing with that letter all that time,

carrying it in the bottom of that dirty bag of his with that stuff? It was that stuff, and not a tear, that had smudged the word love. All those sachets. What strange bedfellows. That letter, he never shared it with her. Why? Her mother did want to love her daughter and her love was thwarted, not by lack of will power, but by her husband, driving his wife to... And then covering it all up for fear of dinting his image. Oh Mam. How I was condemning you too, conditioning you as you were conditioned, as all of society will say. Poor Connie Eames, she was fond of the bottle and drank herself to death. What a tribulation it must have been for her husband, a man of such importance who contributed so greatly to society. What he must have borne.

'Oh Mam. Oh Mam. Oh Mam.' A tear flows for every invocation of the name, and she finds herself rocking on Dermot's bed, cradling herself for the loss of a mother.

And all the time Dermot kept that letter. Why? Why? It is not an inspirational note but a note of utter sadness. But no, there is love in there somewhere, trying to peep out through all her pain. She loved us both dearly. Oh, why did Dermot not tell me? That secret burning him up, enjoined on by his father to keep mum. To keep mum, yes, all to himself, a piece of home – how ironic – a dead piece of home to carry around with him in all his warped wanderings. A suicide note as a talisman, a guide, a motivation, yes, the words, the blue rope, the sea, the death wish.

Oh Dermot, where have you gone? Why are you doing this to me? Have you gone to try once more to follow Mam into obliteration? And was that what drove you to the drugs, not just Mam dying, but the circumstances of her death, that secret you were keeping all the time?

What is she to do? She will go to Charlie. She must. What choice does she have if she wants to locate her brother? And she does, oh she does, despite what Ramón says, she cannot turn her back on her own flesh and blood. She will brave it out, no matter what, and ask Charlie what he knows about her brother.

Chapter Thirty Nine

Not without trepidation does she make her way through the labyrinth, so artificial-looking in daylight with all those lights half-hidden, and trees so obviously planted and pruned to man-made dimensions, and hedges to shape unnatural tunnels. And she thinks she is the nameless character now from her writing who walked in labyrinths in trepidation too. But this is not a time to dwell on such things. She is wearing her duckegg blue jeans with the extra tight zip which gets stuck sometimes and her white cotton blouse (white is always such an unfailing colour in hot countries) buttoned up to the top; it even has long sleeves so as not to give Charlie any ideas, which she would not put past him considering the state of Topless Jane coming out of his room the night of the party, and Gwen saying he roughed her up a bit.

She presses an intercom button. Charlie: what time is it anyway? 4:35 p.m. He should be back by now from entertaining his beach babes. He will take a siesta, no doubt, an old boy like him, at this time of day.

'Yes.' The voice, curt as if interrupted.

'Charlie Eliot?'

'Who wants to know?'

'This is Penelope Eames.'

'Who?'

'A friend of Gwen's.'

The door opens with the creaking of heavy oak reminiscent of a horror movie with no one behind it, and she finds herself in a large hall with high walls bedecked with nude paintings. A Rubens, a Goya, Grande Odalisque by Ingres. Original? Bought or stolen? In front of her is a red door from which low sounds are emanating.

She turns the brass handle into a room of darkness except for a flickering projector flitting shadows on a screen. She looks more closely: a female head, blonde hair, face concealed bobbing on something.

She hears a groan from behind the projector. The film flickers out. The reel runs on until, finally exhausting itself, it comes to a creaky halt.

'Penelope Eames.' She hears the voice from the darkness. It's Charlie's. 'You called at an inopportune moment I'm afraid, my dear.'

'Sorry I...'

'But not to worry,' he says, 'I'll be with you presently. We always get around to things presently.'

During this fraught interim, Penelope ponders on whether to stay or flee. Her impulse is to do the latter but duty, responsibility, sisterly solicitude – her No matter what – forces her to stand her ground.

A moment or two later a side light is switched on and she finds herself surrounded by walls of thick purple curtains with matching lounge couches, and Charlie Eliot on a high wide wicker chair confronts her in Y-fronts and black cotton socks.

'Don't like the cold of Spanish marble,' he says, noticing her looking down. 'I'll put a nice wool carpet down one of these days. We have to consider our actors all. And now let me look at you, my dear. I remember now,' he says musing, 'with Gwenny. Ah yes, but why didn't you come to me before? You're here for the part?'

'No, Charlie, I...'

'Not for the part?'

'No.'

He lifts her hand examining it.

'Sorry I...'

'You saw some of the film?'

'I couldn't help...' she says. She tries to gauge the blind eye. It is the left eye; she is sure of it, by the way it fails to focus, not blinking with more of that dirty white sclera visible.

'So what do you want?' he snaps suddenly, sitting back. 'New passport, new identity, Spanish registration plates for your car?'

'I...'

'Ah,' he says, a finger raised to silence her, 'be careful my dear, loose lips can sink ships, although I must admit, being partial to a little leakage. It adds to the excitement of it all, don't you agree? Everyone knows Charlie. They come to see me before they gamble away their pensions at Mijas racecourse. Buy a passport, my dear [his accent soft again]. The Africans in the beach bars are always looking for passports.'

'Charlie I...'

'You're sure it's not acting you've come about? I have to vet them, you understand. The actors; they come looking, thinking Charlie will make them famous. They all like to be called actors now of course, but I still call the dames actresses. It prevents confusion, wouldn't you agree? He rubs his hand across her buttocks. Penelope winces but is afraid to draw back.

'What a firm little arse. Could you sway it for me?'

'Charlie, I think you misunderstand. I'm not here to...'

'Shh.' The finger to the lips again'

'Look, Charlie...'

'They wanted to extradite me you know, but they can pin nothing on me.' He laughs, creasing up his face. 'I can do things here which Old Bill wouldn't approve of back home. I'm legit, above board,' he says gesticulating effusively. 'People come over here to enjoy the sunshine, you understand, my dear. All those hordes of pink-faced tourists. Are you one of those?'

'No, Charlie. I have a place. I live here.'

'Ah. But will I tell you something now, my dear? Do you think living in sunshine guarantees a happy and long life? You know what I miss?'

'What?' she says tremulously.

'I miss the rain. It's the price I pay – he brushes his hand across his face. A couple of weeks ago, did you see it, the rain coming down cats and dogs? Did you see it?'

'Yes, I saw it.'

'Everyone getting uptight about it. All those holidaymakers with their buckets and spades going around as if their world was falling apart. Building castles in the air. Ha. Well, you know what I did, my dear? Do you?'

'No.'

'Don't just say no, say no, Charlie.'

'No, Charlie.'

'That's better, more polite, don't you think. An Englishman is nothing if not polite. Now where was I?'

'You were going to tell me what you did when it rained... Charlie.'

'I paraded in it. I splashed in it. I strolled around naked with my head upturned to it, drinking in the drops.'

He stops to regard her. Smiles at the look of confused fear on her face. His hand with a ring on each finger is forcing hers upwards along his thigh. 'When the rain hits the John Thomas it's quite a sensation.' She averts her eye when he notices her gaze rising to his off-white Y-fronts with its little protuberance.

'Did you like the paintings,' he says, 'in the hall?'

'I didn't have much time, Charlie, to...'

'They were larger-bottomed in the old days. All those paintings entertaining the royalty; they were the bunny girls of their era. Do you like going to galleries? I like going to galleries,' he says. 'Do you like nudes?'

'I haven't thought about them too much, Charlie.'

202

'It is the greatest thing,' he says, 'to create desire. The artist on his canvas is able to seduce... what I try to do in film.'

What Charlie is, what she is standing before, she knows now, is a caricature of an artist in Y-fronts (if it weren't so sinister it would be risible). 'But to touch,' he is saying, as his free hand brushes against her breast, 'the tactile, is the real thing.'

Having released her hand, he speaks mesmerisingly, opening the top button of her blouse. She stands back... she thinks of the bow-slipping bikini on the beach, wandering hands that should be slapped away. The words she has missed. What is he saying? Something '...lonely, on this earth.' God, this is pathetic. He is sounding like one of those mid-American Bible preachers or those deep toned voiceovers that you hear in documentaries where Penelope always felt one had to be a chain cigarette smoker (or a pipe smoker like her father, for he produced the same authoritative effect in his voice as if there is no dispute: only the truth can emanate from here) to produce such an effect. And here is this Charlie now trying to deliver this fake gravitas for what? For his porn films. God, Ramón is right, so right, but there is Dermot blocking the rescue movement of her hand. Only for Dermot, she could run away.

'Once the mind is captured,' he is saying, 'that region of desire, it can be summoned up, called forth, yes.' He smiles preferring that latter phrase, 'at a moment of desolation. Do you have such moments, my dear? You can tell Charlie. Your friend Gwenny, she told Charlie, and Charlie helped her.'

What business is it of yours? she wants to retort in quick fire but 'Charlie' is what comes out in a pleading tone that disgusts her.

'Shh. Maybe you are too young to know such moments. You don't have the benefit of my disadvantages.'

'Charlie, I came to see you because...'

He waves her again to silence 'Let me tell you about the films, so that you may reconsider. I will pay you well.'

'Charlie...'

'Ah.' He sits back, raises his hands as if for the first time hearing her. 'The lady is about to speak.'

'Charlie, I don't want to know about the films. I want to know about my brother. That's why I came.'

'You came.' He laughs. 'How good it is that you came. I am pleased for you that you came. You came, you saw, but you did not submit.'

'My brother, Charlie.'

'Ah yes, your brother? We all have brothers. This is the thing. Will I tell you about my brother?'

'No, Charlie I...'

'No! You say no?'

'I didn't mean...'

'Why should I want to know about your brother? Fair is fair. Tit for tat. Your tit for my tat. And you have nice tits. Did you have a job done?' He stares, sucking his thumb in and out with exaggerated suction. 'Most of the girls have had a job done except of course for Jane. You know Jane?'

'I have seen her around.'

'Around! Ha. There is nothing round about Jane. You'd have to import parts, to do a job on her.' He laughs. 'But there are compensations with Jane,' he says, 'that boyish figure of hers, most accommodating. What Jane will do for a little polvo blanco. She is a base crazy. You should see her, on her hands and knees, searching for snow on the Sierra Nevada.'

'Please Charlie, let me explain.'

'Explain?' He grabs her fiercely by the hair. 'What could you explain to Charlie?'

'You're hurting me.'

He releases her.

'I want to know about my brother,' she says as boldly as she can, feeling the sting in the roots of her hair, 'Dermot Eames.'

He stares at her in silence for a moment. She blushes, lowering her head, but she forces it up again trying to be bold, trying to outstare him.

'And what makes you think I would know your brother?'

'My brother's gone missing and I wanted to ask you in person if you knew where he might be.'

'Why should Charlie know?'

'He has sold... things to you, Charlie.'

He scowls. 'He told you? The squealing scumbag told you that?'

Oh God, what is she to do. She has just informed on her brother.

'Charlie, I'm worried about him.'

'Come closer,' he commands.

She draws nearer, getting a stale, spent smell from him.

'Closer.'

He reaches for her face. She tries with all her might not to grimace as he presses with stubby thumb and forefinger on either side of her mouth, hurting her with his rings.

'You have a sensuous mouth,' he says and he squeezes harder, but she does not cry out.

He releases her mouth and, as it falls back into its undistorted shape, he raises her right hand which involuntarily was clenched, and opening the fingers, brings it close to his face. 'And such long nails.'

'Charlie, I want to know...'

'Of course you want to know, and I will tell you.' He stares into her eyes. 'The big fish swallow the minnow, you know that?'

'I don't understand you, Charlie.'

'The minnow,' he says, 'they are just delivery boys, whey-faced weanlings. I pick up the phone and dial a coke and they come running, ha, with their tails between their legs. The tales they tell [his tone now of foreboding], the lies they unfold. But see, my dear, I am the big fish and I do the payoffs, good and bad you know, big and small, temporary and... final.'

He pauses, stares coldly at her. 'If they doublecross, if they don't deliver the good shit. You know, the good shit?'

'No Charlie, I don't.'

'Things have to be pure for Charlie. Like you, dear,' he says sniffing at her. 'Are you pure?'

'Charlie, I...'

'Otherwise it's...' and he draws his finger across his throat...'kaput.'

He sits back interlocking his fingers. 'So, my dear,' he says, returning to his avuncular tone, 'perhaps we can come to an agreement. You were a little hesitant initially, were you not?'

'Sorry, Charlie.'

'This matter of your brother gives it a double bind, don't you think?'

'I have no acting experience, Charlie.'

'It can be taught,' he says. He looks her up and down. 'You have the requisites. As well as the language. My girls from Russia, my girls from Africa, they all speak, but only the one language, the international language of grunts and groans. But you could have a more specific part; it would be like coming from the silent era. You like the silent era? You like the Keystone Cops?'

'Yes, Charlie but...'

'They're the only cops I take seriously.'

'Charlie I...'

'We could have real scripts with real words. You are a writer, if I remember.'

206

How did he know that? Oh yes, how well he remembered at the party Gwen introducing her to him as such.

'You could write the plot,' he says, 'under my direction of course. I get bored with all the repetition. I want something with a bit more originality. A story line; not just the sex, but sex with a story line. Could you do it, do you think, my dear? Many writers star in their own scripts.'

'Charlie, I'm not that sort of writer.'

'Oh. What sort of writer are you then?' he says snappily. 'Do you not put sex in your novels? They must be very, very dry. I think you will write that script,' he says icily. 'Anyway,' he says rising, 'that's the deal. Could you be good enough now to hand me my trousers.' She reaches for his dun-coloured linen trousers draped on the couch. 'You make the film,' he says inserting a leg, 'and I might consider letting your brother off the hook.'

'What do you mean, hook? What hook is he on Charlie?'

'Go away now,' he says dismissively, 'and think about my offer.'

'But what did he do on you Charlie?'

'He's an adulterer.'

'An adulterer! How could he be?'

'Adulterers, they freeze my waters. But now,' he says fastening his belt, 'I've got things to do. Come back tomorrow. The offer will end at...' He looks at his watch.

'High noon,' she says.

He glares. 'Don't shit with me, my dear. Tomorrow morning, ten o'clock on the navel.'

Chapter Forty

Coming out of the villa, she sees Ramón on the far side of the street. Was he waiting? No, he is just passing by on his way to the beach in his lifeguard gear, blue and yellow jacket and shorts, recouping the days lost – were they lost, those days? Why was he cold towards her when she told him she was going to see Charlie? He became so distant; made her wonder was he really what he was: that gentle sensitive man she was growing so fond of. And Gwen always going on about someone who is not of their own sort, doesn't help either. She calls after him. He hadn't noticed her – not even from the corner of his eye? 'Ramón,' she calls louder. He turns but doesn't smile; he wants to get away from here. Away from her? Can that be true? Back to his girlfriends on the beach, the new contingent just arrived (she saw them the other evening, already boisterous with their suitcases in the vestibule).

'Let's sit down here,' she says seizing a chair at an outdoor café table. He says nothing except 'Do you want a cup of tea?' A cup of tea. Was there ridicule in his tone? It was like saying you Irish and English can solve the world's problems over a cup of tea. She at least expected him to enquire how she got on with Charlie. The café is noisy. He orders tea for her. He will have nothing. He sits aloof in front of her, avoiding her stare, looking at people passing by.

'Ramón, talk to me,' she says reaching for his hand. 'What we had, those few days, what we gave each other.' He keeps looking at the people walking up and down the street, coming and going from the beach where he should be now, she knows.

'You were in there,' he says eventually, pointing towards the villa.

'I had to.'

'With that hijo de puta.'

'What?'

'Never mind.'

'Ramón, I was...'

'I have to go,' he says. 'There is no one at my post.'

'What am I going to do, Ramón?'

'I told you what not to do,' he says rising. 'So why ask me when you don't heed my advice? I told you...' and he nods towards the villa... 'that place is bad.'

'I know it's bad but...'

'Bad things happen there.'

'But Ramón, my brother...'

He walks away.

His silence is saying: there is nothing more he can do. He is going towards the sea, mingling, losing himself (losing her, or more accurately she is losing him) in the crowds, on his way now to guard or save someone else's life.

Should she run after him? Oh, why is everyone not letting her speak? She wants to confide in him, to talk to him; she desperately needs to talk to him but he has gone. What is she to do?

Ten on the navel. Who would have thought this could happen to her, and that it's not a clip from some old movie with the projector and its rickety sound flickering the grainy celluloid in that room? What does Charlie want of her? Is he serious? Does he really think she will perform (act is hardly the word) in a porn movie? Does he really think she would do such a thing? But he doesn't know her. He just knows the flesh, the piece of ass, the what-you-see-is-what-you-get, as they say. It is preposterous, the whole thing, but what he holds over her, if it is true about his power, and Dermot implied it, practically admitted it in his last outburst, to the adulteration of the cocaine. Oh, and she in her naïveté thinking of adultery only in the context of marriage. An adulterer: one who contaminates the lives of others, one who is not true, one who is not constant. Oh, what is she to do?

The police, she ponders as she walks; she will go to the police. But no, how can she go there?

She returns to her apartment. She craves security, four walls at least around her, to think, and not the openness of a beach with all its distractions, and Ramón there too of course. It is better to leave matters lie between them for a while. Oh, how is she going to contact Dermot? What is she to do? Everything is going pearshaped. Ramón wants her to stay away from Charlie. It is understandable, especially in the context of his mother's death – perfectly, perfectly understandable. And Ramón saved her brother's life. She cannot fault him. But what he demands now is impossible. Oh, men and their demands. He is asking her to turn her back on her own brother. And, as for Charlie, he is asking her to prostitute herself for her brother. Oh, what is she to do? This quandary, it is so difficult to deal with in real life. If it were in a novel – the whole blasted thing – she would have found a resolution; she could be dispassionate; she would be able to think clearly. No, she can't do what Ramón asks of her? Is blood thicker than water?

She will go back to Charlie, no matter what? She will be more firm with him the next time. No more aborted sentences. She will finish what she wants to say. Compel him by the force of her language to listen. To brush away that silencing finger of his. Oh God, how like her father he is. He will try to subjugate her. But she... she could threaten to expose him. Ha, he would love that. He will laugh at her and crush her like powerful men can do. He will call her bluff, for no armaments has she to confront him with other than the weak limbs of a female. He will have his way with her, but will it be her? Will it be Penelope Eames who will be violated, or will it be the image of her? A splicing of celluloid to get the curves, the bottom, the tits, the sway of the hips, the walk, the lying down, the thighs nicely parted, just right, all under the flickering image of a rickety projector, the growing excited, and – think of it – the service she will provide in darkened rooms all over the world, the rapes she will prevent, her image to gratify lonely men.

Was that what Charlie was on about in his warped way, with his lonely of the earth spiel, trying to justify his actions? She sees the woman in the film performing her. She is Penelope. She is acting and creating at the same time just as Charlie wanted, making herself up as she goes along. Along where? Along the path of ruin, the violation of all that is pure. She is sitting with pen and paper writing, looking up now and again to see how her alter ego is getting on, then looking down again to write amendments to the scene. What amendments? What improvements; a bit more passion here, more exposure there, the story line, what's it about? Body parts of course: a breast is talking sotto voce to a mouth, the buttocks are deep in conversation with a hand, the head is nodding in agreement to a torso, and the inevitable conflict occurs now between the various parts vying for hegemony in the film. And there is Charlie on his throne, his director's chair, looking on approvingly, with his name etched on its canvas back.

And she asks herself, is that too bad? Is that too much to give for her brother's life (for she is convinced it is a death threat that is hanging over him). Even though to Ramón, it appeared that Dermot did not want to save his own life, but it was Charlie who was driving him to such an extreme. It is clear now. Removing Charlie's threat will save Dermot's life.

So perhaps it won't be so bad; she could endure it. Women have endured worse through the centuries (What about that naked slave girl in the painting on Charlie's wall? What did she endure?). To save her brother, to lose her lover. Oh Ramón, you saw so clearly what was involved. And who are these actors she would be expected to perform with? Topless Jane no doubt, and God knows who else, and the spectre of gonorrhoea, syphilis, AIDS, loom before her in great Technicolor blobs, and her own life, her chance, perhaps her only chance of happiness, to be sacrificed: her life for Dermot's.

But even then – and her hesitation returns – are there guarantees that Charlie Eliot will keep his word?

Chapter Forty One

She will talk to Gwen. The sun is setting and the multicoloured lights are on around the pool as she glances out the balcony, but there is no light from Gwen's window. Still, she could be resting. She goes out to the corridor and rings her doorbell. There is no reply. She hurries downstairs (too impatient to take the lift) to the reception desk. They may know where she is. Gwen often talked to the girls there, but today it is a dusky-looking male manning the desk

'I'm enquiring about Gwen...?

'Who?'

'Room 306.' God, she just realises she doesn't even know her surname.

'Oh yes,' he says, 'you are Ms Eames?'

'Yes.'

'There's a letter for you from la señora Morris.'

'Morris?'

'Yes. She had to return to England urgently.'

Return to England. Urgently. What is all this urgency about Gwen?

She hurries back to her apartment; pours herself a glass of tinto and sits on the tubular chair on the darkening balcony overlooking the lights of the pool. The bar below is abuzz with the early evening drinkers, as she reads:

Dear Penelope,

Excuse this scribbled note, but I'm being forced away I'm afraid. Good-bye Spain. You were right it seems after all about looking after one's skin. I didn't heed your warning. The thing is I've developed facial melanoma. It was discovered when I went to Dr Grayson, when you were away, to get something for that lingering cold (the price I paid for that cold!). I'd prefer to have one of our own treat it back home. Anyway, a climate sometimes can get too hot, don't you think?

I decided to leave this way without fuss before you returned. You were my best china, you know. I wish you well with your Spanish beau. It took me a long time, didn't it, to discover how many Fs are in good-bye?

Gwen.

'Oh no, Gwen,' she exclaims putting the letter down. 'I was never trying to get rid of you. Was I? I never told you to go away. Was it some variance, some gesture of mine? I wanted you to be my friend. But that was not enough for you.'

The music and the merrymaking grow louder down below. She thinks of the sun, that two-faced God dispensing good and evil like so many things, like us. Dark side, bright side, the dark side of every brightness. But what is that noise now? Young, screeching girls with their first sunburn, oblivious, letting their hair down early; they're high on something; on top of the world. And she knows now that she is alone. Never before, even when in Ireland, did she feel this cutting aloneness as strongly and in the midst of all this revelry. How strange the world is.

What time is it? Nearly two a.m. She must have dozed. She has a crick in her neck. It's quiet down below now. The revellers have taken themselves off somewhere, probably to La Caverna. She opens her laptop but becomes sleepy again and finds herself following that girl once more down the quiet road, twisting by the field with the dead tree and the blue rope swaying. But this time it is not empty at its noose; this time it contains a head, the head of a woman, the contorted face of her mother.

She screams. How uncharacteristic it is for her to suffer such things, for she was never one to have nightmares. Her terrors were always conscious. Nightmares are Dermot's domain. How many times had she comforted him as a child? He still needs her. She realises. The dream is telling her. Their mother is dead. And Dermot is carrying her death around with him, afraid, unwilling to let her go. Despite everything, despite all the loud posturing, Dermot is still clinging to the umbilical cord. No matter how weak it may have been, it was still their link of love. But there is only her now to look out for him; she, being the elder, is the saviour sibling. There is no one else. It would be unfair to trouble Ramón again on the matter. He has saved a life. He moves on, but he doesn't understand that it is not over. There is more to it. But it is her role now to try to save a life that, despite Charlie, perhaps does not want to be saved. This will be done. She will have fulfilled her duty. Her conscience will be salved. She will then be truly free.

Her mobile phone rings that overture – she still hasn't got around to changing it – quite knocking the thoughts out of her head.

'Wakey wakey.'

'Sheila.' Oh no, not Sheila, not now. What time is it? She looks at the bedside clock: 9:05. She had conked out. God. A panic seizes her. She had fully intended to use those quiet dawn hours to plan her course of action. She is all in a flux. Less than an hour, that's all she has left to make her decision, To change a life, to save a life, to destroy a life.

'Penelope, are you there?'

'Yes, Sheila.'.

'That interview you did...'

Oh God, is she going to say there was something wrong with that too?

'I'm just ringing to tell you it will be in next week's colour mag of *The Female on Sunday.* Is that great news or what?'

'Yes, it is great news. Thank you, Sheila.'

'They got some terrific shots of you. Wait till you see them. Needless to say I had to push them on it. They were inclined to leave it for a while; they were trying to slot in one of those nonentities from Reality TV. Penelope, you're still there?'

'Sorry. Yes, Sheila.'

'Your fans want to know what you're up to over there. We gotta give them what they want on Penelope Eames, their favourite novelist. What, what?'

'Stop it, Sheila. Stop flattering me.'

'How is the new baby coming along?'

'It's coming along,' Penelope says, watching the minute hand move on the clock, feeling her pulse rate increase accordingly. Is there a ratio between time moving and panic seizing? How many accelerating beats can a heart take before it selfdestructs?

'No excuse,' Sheila says, 'with all that sun and patio lifestyle. I expect you bring your laptop onto your porch and watch the red sunsets.'

'Look, Sheila I've got to go.'

'You're sure you're okay?'

'I'm fine.'

'You sound, well...Oh maybe I got you too early.'

'No, not too early.'

'No?'

'It's just I have an appointment at ten and I have to look my best.'

'An appointment? Ah,' Sheila says, 'I bet he's a hunk.'

216

She showers, dresses in what? What will she wear? Clothes are a language, they speak, they express not just who you are but what your intentions are. She thinks of Tiffany Pringle and the photographer as she dries her hair with her white towel. What instructions they gave: what to wear, how to wear it, what hemline, what cleavage to reveal. All relevant of course, she muses sardonically, to her written words? She slips into a short cotton white skirt. He can interpret it as he wishes, she decides, stepping into high heels and raising her arms to receive her black top. Yes, she has decided then, but she does not know what to expect, what to really expect. Could it be like one of those visits to the doctor to get a jab – if she closes her eyes she won't feel the pain. Let her imagination anaesthetise her. Can it be much worse than the photo session she endured? Oh yes it can, for there will be third parties involved poking at her, exploring her orifices, sniffing about her like dogs. Oh God, what will be done to her for her brother's sake?

She prances like a zoo animal up and down outside the gate to Charlie's villa, drawing curious stares from passersby, glancing at her watch every couple of minutes, smoking her Marlboro cigarettes – that's how many this morning? She can't remember; the packet is running low; she'll have to buy another just to have on reserve in case... in case what? Oh dear, it is a quarter to ten already.

The time has come. She stomps out a half-smoked cigarette and applies an atomiser to her wrists – she is already beginning to sweat (how she'd prefer to be down by the seafront at this moment with a cool breeze in her hair), for the sun is high now beaming down, no longer on poor Gwen, alas. How many Fs are in good-bye? The phrases she had. And Charlie too, he has phrases. And Ramón, he would be writing all those idioms down, and she sighs, if it were a perfect world.

The gate is open. He is expecting her, or has someone preceded her? She walks up, retracing her steps of the labyrinthine path. There is a fork to the path leading to the right, which she hadn't noticed before, almost concealed by eucalyptus trees. She glances that way; something catches her attention: a plank, yes that's what it is, lying across the path. She moves closer pushing the foliage aside; it's a newly made path, of concrete, unlike the rest of the labyrinth of binding gravel and sand. It's fresh still in its original white-grey look, only now congealing. And there are little dots in it. She remembers footpaths being made on the streets in her childhood. How some of the kids used to put their mark (when the pathmaker had gone away leaving them to dry), a hand, a finger, names engraved in the cement before it dried. And here too were little signs: single dots, hardly the paw marks of an animal; a cat's talons, for example, would constitute a cluster. But theses were single, individual indentations.

She turns back towards the villa. She sees Topless Jane at the front door stooping down to wipe her pointed heels with a tissue. What a dolt, not watching where she treads. She looks around as if to gauge where to dislodge the tissue, but then decides to put it in her handbag. She takes out lipstick which she holds like a jutting penis ready to assault her lips. Who invented these things? Penelope wonders. Could they not have lip paint come out another way other than as solid out of a sheath? She never thought of lipstick like that before. Why is such vulgar imagery, at this moment, blitzing her mind? Is the problem with her, or are these things just fortuitously phallic? It's the way her mind is working now with sleazy Charlie looming. Yes, that's it, she concludes, it's the way her world is being coloured. And Jane, in a

218

skimpy micro skirt and frilly red blouse, is standing on the raised wooden porch. She doesn't see Penelope Eames coming through the shrubbery. Pressing her lips tightly, she returns the lipstick to her handbag and pushes the intercom button. Is she one of the actresses? Penelope wonders as Jane disappears behind the door. Now it is time for Penelope Eames to come forward. Oh, how she'd love to turn heel (seeing as she is on the subject of heels) and run away.

She pushes the intercom button. There is no answering voice this time, but the door opens as before with the same ominous groan.

The film projector is flickering. Topless Jane is kneeling, her head nodding on Charlie's lap while he sits on his throne. Light glimmering, dim, dim, curtains drawn, difficult to see. And the old black and white, the speed of the celluloid turning. Did it happen? What you thought happened? A blur; a groan. The image and the real.

'Ah, the lady of the beautiful nails.'

Topless Jane raises her head without the slightest embarrassment. It is more a look of curiosity: who has come to visit? In the dimmed light everything appears sickly with stale smells of God knows what in a windowtight room. And the curtains, are they ever taken down and cleaned? There is dust – she can see it in the shafts of light stealing through, and in all the corners in a daguerreotype, a sepia world, in such contrast to the blazing sun outside. Early erotica, that's what he's trying to capture, she is convinced, like the clandestine world of Victorians. She follows it now. But where are the other 'actors'? Is it just Topless Jane in her unspoken role? Does she recognise her, or is it that she is already blown out of her mind? Base crazy, as Charlie said. Her concentration is totally taken up with Charlie like an expectant dog's, rather than regarding Penelope now, after that initial cursory glance. Topless Jane sifts excitedly as Charlie produces the mirror tray, placing it on his lap, and she and he use the straws just as Gwen had done. He pushes her down again, holds her by the hair. 'Oh Charlie,' she pleads (her first words, her only words) as her roots are being pulled (just as he had done earlier to Penelope). He pushes her aside, the pet animal he has grown tired of, and Penelope waits with dread, wondering what will happen next. He is like some fickle emperor, who growing quickly wearisome of one game, soon wants to play another.

'We must welcome the lady of the beautiful nails,' Charlie says. 'She is waiting in the wings.'

Topless crawls towards him. 'She's not as good as me, Charlie.'

'Shut up,' he says, and he lashes out with his foot, kicking her away.

'You said there would be other actors,' Penelope says trying to conceal her anger at such humiliation.

'Ah yes,' Charlie says, 'we will have the actors.' And he glances at Topless Jane who is crouched down sniffing the last of the powder off the mirror. 'When one has only one eye to arouse,' he says, 'one needs compensatory addenda.'

He looks at her. She knows he wants her to enquire about his eye, but she says nothing. She will not give him the satisfaction. He continues. 'You know,' he says taking her hand, 'how I lost the sight of my eye? It was taken from me. Someone with long nails just like yours. You wouldn't do that to Charlie, now would you, Penelope Eames?' And he draws her nails towards his right eye. 'Would you put out the sight of Samson?'

Samson! God his megalomania knows no bounds. She could burst out laughing if only... and she thinks of her father and

Victor Mature.

'She claimed I was too demanding of her, a Ukrainian Delilah. Would you believe it? Ha. But the truth is I wasn't demanding enough.'

'Charlie, I...'

Still holding her hand, he puts his right forefinger to his lips. 'There are options we can discuss.'

'Options?'

'For the script. Shall we tentatively title it A Threesome?'

'What about my brother?' Penelope says.

He exhales. 'Why talk about him at a moment like this?'

'I want to know. Please, Charlie.'

Charlie snaps as if tiring of the charade. 'That scumbag was too soft,' he growls. 'He needed hardening.'

She has done it now, ruined things, couldn't help herself; she recoiled and ran out the door when he pressed with those demands in sheer naked lust with all the games over ('You fancy a bit of rough, my dear?'). And what have they done to Dermot? God, what had they already done to him perhaps, rendering her negotiations with Charlie obsolete? She thinks back on the making of the footpath in her childhood, just outside their house in Dundrum. A new path, she remembers built by the County Council after a big truck had broken the old one. So she went out in the twilight of a winter evening. She remembers it was winter because of the early darkness and because the pathmaker had strewn some sacking over the path to prevent frost damage. And she ventured forth out her gate. How brave and daring she felt, the thrill – positively subversive – as she crouched under the swan-necked street lamp. And she inscribed the letters while the screed was still wet. The D with the little squiggle and P with a flourish, done more with her nail than her finger, for even then her nails were long. All completed before her father came home. He would not see it till the morning, when the cement would have hardened, too late then to undo her work. What a triumph it would be for her over him. It would be like an emblem or something hardened for posterity, and not a thing would he ever be able to do about it (for undoubtedly he would have reprimanded her action as wilful damage to property). As it turned out he never even noticed it – the letters were small – which was a bit of a disappointment for her in a way afterwards.

But there they were, those initials, of her brother and herself, hardening through the night. Hardening, she says aloud as if only now discovering the word. Hardening, she says again, with a sudden shiver of recognition. What Charlie had said, the word, about Dermot. Hardening, he said, he needed hardening. And she realises with terror what it all means. Hardening, the path in Charlie's, the fresh cement. And she cries out, 'Dermot, good God!'

He meets her at the fountain, having phoned her on her mobile. He said little, just a contrite tone of, 'Could I see you?' He sits anxiously on the low lip of the fountain, looking left and right to see from which sidestreet she would hail. It was her decision to meet him there. She did not want him to come to the apartment, where the police would be further bothering her. She had tipped them off. They were incredulous at first, but they became more convinced as she spoke to them in Spanish, as her tears flowed. '¿Su hermano?' They had to check it out. With power drills they dug up the body. They found Dermot, bound: hands, legs and mouth taped.

She should not have looked. They wanted her to turn away, a gentle lady officer trying to steer her from the scene; but she insisted, just to be sure that it was... And then she turned away. How did she contain herself as she witnessed the corpse of her brother with his eyes frozen in terror staring out at her through a blood-congealed face? She does not know. It was like she was holding herself in with a big tight girdle all the time it took to see the whole sorry business through.

And then when it was over, the floodgates opened. She was alone, bereft, wandering the streets of Felicidad, refusing the police offer of custodial care. She wanted to break away but did not want to be alone. Oh, she cursed the contradiction in herself. People stopped to look at her, at the weeping woman with dishevelled hair just about avoiding collisions with cars and people. Children with their buckets and spades and surf boards and Lilos came to a standstill on footpaths to behold this woman passing by. Was this in the travel brochures? No more than the rain. And then just at the nadir point she felt the throbbing of her mobile phone in her pocket, like someone else's heart beating.

He rises when he sees her, embraces her. 'I read about it in the newspaper,' he says. 'I am so, so sorry.'

She sobs. 'Oh Ramón, was he buried alive? I could not bring myself to ask the police. I felt that if I spoke at all to them after they discovered Dermot... I felt if I opened my mouth at that stage I would...'

'It's okay,' he says.

Her tears fall on his shoulder, darkening his white cotton shirt. He's soaking it up, her sorrow.

'Don't think of it now,' he says, 'it's over.'

'What he must've gone through.'

'It's finished now. His pain, it's gone.'

'At least they got him,' she says sniffling, 'that Charlie Eliot.'

'Yes,' he says, 'at least that.'

He pushes back her hair that's moistening over her eyes. 'I was at fault, Penelope,' he says. 'I thought you were going to sell yourself cuerpo y alma to... that man.'

'Oh Ramón, I...'

'No. Let me finish. I feared for you. I had such little belief. I kept thinking of drug addicts and drug pushers and what they had done to my mother. And what... what they could do to you.'

'Oh God.'

'It's okay.' He kisses her, vacuums up her tears, but they keep flowing again, like the fountain unceasing.

'It will take time... a long time, but it will heal, the pain that you feel now.'

'What did he feel?' she cries out.

An elderly blackshawled woman approaches them and, seeing the tears rolling down Penelope's face, offers her a packet of tissues which she had taken from her handbag.

'La pobrecita.'

'Gracias, señora,' Ramón says taking the tissues.

225

'De nada.'

He dabs her eyes.

'People are so kind,' she sobs. 'How is it, Ramón, that people are so kind?'

'The world is not all bad.'

'But how could they do that to him, such a thing, to another human being? No matter what,' her voice breaks, 'he was my brother?'

'It's over, over, and the wound you have, it will heal, I promise you it will heal. Like with my mother, the wound has healed in me. When I met you it had begun, and I didn't realise...'

'You didn't realise what?' she simpers.

'How you had helped me.'

'How had I helped you?'

'By being you.'

'Oh, Ramón.' She finds that familiar nook, so firm and warm, between his shoulder and his neck.

And he repeats the words wound and heal and 'it will be all right but only in time,' and the words, as the world goes by, become like a little mantra or lullaby soothing her.

'Maybe it's because I never had a brother or sister,' he says as her sobbing subsides into a gentler rhythm. 'I didn't understand the bond that attached you to Dermot. I'd go to the beach pretending that I could block you out with my work, with other people, but all the time I was... I was...'

'You were what?'

'In there with you. Feeling your pain.'

She raises her head to look into his face, his caring eyes. 'If I hadn't come to Spain that would not have happened to him.'

'Oh no,' he says, 'he was coming anyway. That is the way they work, people who are dealing in drugs; they are always looking for bigger markets.'

'But if I had compromised myself with Charlie, if I had agreed to do what he demanded... the first time I went to see him, if I had... I mean, then... then Dermot could still be alive.'

'No,' Ramón says pressing her to him. 'Charlie would not have saved Dermot's life.'

'The pain,' she cries out, 'the pain he must've suffered. It's unthinkable. God!'

'There was nothing you could do. Nothing, ¿comprendes? The white powder owned him. And no matter what you would've done for Charlie, it would've made no difference. Giving yourself to him would've just made two tragedies out of one. You did everything humanly possibly for him.'

'Oh still, Ramón.'

He cradles her head in his arms, soothing her. 'Draw breath, draw breath,' he whispers, 'it's over.'

They sit for a while at the fountain until the church bell rings – the brass gong heaving on ropes. They rise and, wordlessly, are drawn towards the sound, his great arm cocooning her as they make their way up the hill. They enter the dark interior of the church, lit only by a huddle of candles near the altar. There is a wonderful coolness in the air. They walk down the marble aisle, in silence, for there is no one as yet in the church – no mumblers or bead rattlers to distract them. Penelope, with his hand to steady hers, puts a coin in the candle box and lights a candle. They stand there, staring and staring until the candle waxes faint, and a new colour looms before them – candle blue, in the dying of the flame.

Chapter Forty Five

She is doing her breast check. Sitting in her pyjama bottoms on the dralon stool at the vanity mirror, she commences to go through the five points.

Know what's normal for you.

Look and feel. What do those implant women feel like, touching silicone? The scar is almost invisible now.

Know what changes to look for. Devil a bit. But wait, the right breast, underneath, what is it? It feels like a little pea, caught there under her skin. She feels. Oh God, it is a lump.

She hadn't wanted to tell him that night in the pensión in Seville. When they stood somewhat embarrassedly (for her part at least) in front of each other, and yet their nakedness seemed natural. Her arms were crossed with virginal bashfulness on her breasts initially, and he said she was Venus from that Botticelli painting rising out of the seashell like a priceless pearl, except for her hair of course which was not as long and was limited in what it could conceal. But he lifted her arms slowly, gently away, and he saw her and they saw each other and when one thought in such a furnace – it was up to ninety Fahrenheit – with the whirring fan like an equatorial breeze saying it was all right (breathing Venus into life) to be like that, to stand like that in such a swelter; it was the natural thing. Still there was that awkwardness, and she was trembling despite the heat. But he was enraptured – the word he used. Her beauty that she was so unsure of – how could she be otherwise when it was never measured? – if beauty can be measured or tested. But in its rawness enrapturing him: the springy hair between her legs, the pale buttocks in their bare revelation, the defects of vein visible in her right calf, all those things, all raw flesh, no matter how beautiful or disguised one may be for the colour magazines, we're all primates deep down. But he was enraptured and he saw no flaw, no defect, bathed as he was in the sublime image he possessed of her.

But the second lump. This new discovery. Oh yes, she will tell him, but not now. Why mar these retrieved moments? This love that resurrected out of a death, out of Dermot in the concrete. Can good really spring from evil, as Ramón maintains? Must sacrifices be made for the gods as in ancient times in expiation for our sins? Oh, how is she thinking like this? What has set her on this tangent to consider Dermot so, as an instrument, a means to an end for her, to secure a happiness on this earth, that he was the price to pay? Oh, banish the thought. But everything, as Ramón says, is weighted. And she locates the lump once more, definitely pea-size. Such a little thing to weigh one down amidst the resuscitated delight she was marvelling in now with the growing intimacy between them. Events carry more weight than the self. She will tell Ramón that when they are back in his little house, his casita, their new-found Bower of Bliss.

Oh, it's so sacred, so fragile this thing called human love. And that distress signal from Dermot, a blaring klaxon in all their lives that shattered the eureka moment she had spent all her life seeking.

But human and not divine love is all she can aspire to, all she can expect, despite Ramón's rapture about Venus, the analogy, sprung from his ardour, is the male passion carried hyperbolically, she knows; she has learned that and does not love him any less for it. But when the morning comes there will be – what she prefers – equilibrium in their love, that is to say without too many highs or those fearful crashing lows – something more constant than the fluttering wings of desire. She is not greedy. On the contrary, she is grateful for what she has. And he is a man after all, and she cannot expect too much of him, and she as a woman cannot be that... delicate, intimate – she is searching for the word – in the dénouement of her naked self, her most visceral self; yes, that is the word.

And that second time he never noticed, carried away as he was in the throes, her breasts he fondled and kissed and swooned over, and she all the time fearing (but not wishing to steer him away) where that finger would touch, something hard like the stone in a plum, and not soft and supple like a breast should be. And yes, breast is a metonym in the male mind for woman. And his not knowing as he swooned, and she was there for him as she thought she always would be.

But it may be nothing after all, nothing worth the telling, involving just another little cut and scar that time will heal. And for now she has things to do: a coffin to fly home, a funeral to arrange, a failed father to sort out – yes, that residual husk of a man, floundering with drool on his collar, raging against his own impotence, she is ready to sort out now.

Sheila phoned while she was packing, talking her usual nineteen to the dozen. Penelope never got to tell her, never got a word in edgeways, about Dermot or indeed about finding the second lump. Besides, Sheila would not have followed such things; they would be perceived as deviations in the ongoing romance of life. And as for her writing, yes she will write again, but true to her new found self now. Sheila will not like it no more than she liked her article on the Costa expats, that was brushed aside as a temporary hitch; but it wasn't a temporary hitch; it was the start of something; Penelope knows that now.

And she thinks – no longer with the old fear – of that girl in her story: she is on a journey into a cave, a womb perhaps for a reversal of her birth so that she can start again and come out into the light, that bright Spanish light, warm and welcoming.